Journey Into Hope

Edited By
Rachel Connelly

Black Mare Books

First Edition 2025

This is a work of fiction. Names, characters, places, brands, media, and incidents are either the product of the author's imagination or are used fictitiously. The author acknowledges the trademarked status and trademark owners of various products referenced in this work of fiction, which have been used without permission. The publication/use of these trademarks is not authorized, associated with, or sponsored by the trademark owners.

ISBN: 978-1-959008-98-9

Copyeditor – Alicia Richardson

Developmental Editor – Rachel Connelly

Cover Design – Arthur Doweyko

Interiors – Alicia Richardson

A LETTER FROM THE EDITOR

Each year, we pick a different theme for these anthologies, and this is a particularly timely one. In an age of so much division and tension, we're all searching for hope. Hope for a better tomorrow, hope for peace, hope for progress. And though it may seem elusive, the beautiful thing about hope is that it can be found just about anywhere.

When we set the guidelines for this contest, authors are given free rein over genre and style—but they must address the theme in some way. And in every single submission, each author found and led us to hope in a different place. Some took us to fantastical worlds with frightening creatures, where hope is found in an adventurous quest. Some introduced us to slices of life, where hope is found in a family's shared laughter or in taking a chance on a new lifestyle. Others still brought us with them into their deepest, most personal depths, showing us that hope can even be found there—soft and vulnerable, and yet fiercely powerful.

I am immensely proud of every single author in this anthology. I always tell my authors that my job as a developmental editor is not to change their story, or to take it and mold it into something shiny and sterile and perfect. My job is to identify their unique voice and give them the tools to amplify it—to make sure their story gets told while remaining authentically theirs. I think in this anthology, you'll find ten individual personalities shining bright as they take their turns in the spotlight to show us what's in their heart. Ten unique settings where they have discovered hope lives.

A big thank you to everyone at the Houston Writers Guild, Women in the Visual and Literary Arts, and Inklings Publishing for making this anthology possible. Their dedication to lifting up our local writers and giving them a platform to share their work is unmatched. The Houston writing scene is infinitely richer thanks to their contributions.

Thank you also to our wonderful judges for reading all the outstanding submissions and helping us curate the selection you see here. And to our incredible editing and publishing team, led by the magnificent Fern Brady, for working closely with our authors and guiding their words across the finish line.

Finally, this anthology could not exist without every author who took the time to submit their stories to us. Whether or not your piece made it into the published collection, we are endlessly thankful to everyone who allowed us into their worlds and trusted our team with their creations. Every single one of you is incredibly, uniquely talented, and it is our greatest joy to bear witness to your creative journey.

—Rachel Connelly, Developmental Editor

P.S. Another massive thank you goes to the authors for never making me chase them down over deadlines, which is often like herding giant artsy cats who have grown-up day jobs and real lives outside of this anthology. Thank you for reading and responding to your emails in a timely fashion. Seriously. You're all rock stars and it was a pleasure to work with each of you.

Contents

The Robot and the Green Dragon

by Denise Bossarte (Honorable Mention)

Part I.

It began on the first day of spring.

D974-T92's day at the Mainichi Japanese Daily newspaper began as usual. It was the first run of the special spring edition of the newspaper, which had seeds embedded within each of its pages. It was a tradition to print the Green newspapers at the start of spring. Once planted, they would grow into flowers to attract butterflies and other pollinators. Next week's edition would even have herbs that could be grown to eat.

D974-T92 was the floor supervisor overseeing the multiple C62Wz's working the newspaper plant. D974-T92's job was to make sure that the presses ran smoothly, and that the newspapers were bundled and loaded into the self-driving trucks to be delivered to the other cities on Hokkaido Island, and to the other islands by plane.

D974-T92's position was actually more of an honorable retirement. As a robotic hero of the 2062 Chikara tsunami and Haruki nuclear power plant disaster, they were granted their position as a sign of respect. An honor for what they had done to prevent a complete breach of the Haruki reactor and their efforts in leading the robotic teams' cleanup after the tsunami.

For a human, theirs would have been a posh job working at the historic newspaper, the pride of Japan. The C62Wzs required little oversight. Although limited in their capabilities, they were very efficient in the functionalities they were designed and programmed for. A human would have enjoyed the minimal effort required to fill the role. For D974-T92, it was mind-numbingly boring.

Over the years, they had tried many ways to keep themselves engaged and their intellect busy. Eventually, they settled on the practice of origami. The physicality of folding the thin paper was not a significant challenge to their dexterous fingers, but they found the process of following the elaborate patterns captivating. The Robotic Treaties required that their nanites cover their metal alloy frame and limbs with flesh-like "skin" whenever they were out of their home, particularly when traveling to and from work. They understood this was to make the D974-T robots less threatening to humans and the skin did not interfere with their work or their hobby.

They had spent their days conceiving more and more intricate origami designs, foldings that took dozens or even hundreds of iterations to reveal a final creation. Their works were in museums throughout Japan. And multiples of their designs have been implemented in constructing more resilient buildings to withstand future tsunamis.

But on this day, things shifted when they pulled a sample paper from the conveyor belt to review its quality. It was traditional for the edition of the first day of spring to be focused on environmental stewardship and greening efforts. They were startled to see a picture taken of themselves standing next to the Haruki nuclear power plant right after the 2062 Chikara tsunami. They were positioned at the front of the Haruki-Chikara robotic teams, as they later became known, which had done the majority of the work with recovery, reclamation, and restoration of the city of Akkeshi and the Kushiro Subprefecture.

They had intentionally ignored dates over the years, particularly any anniversary dates of the Haruki-Chikara disasters. They read the bold headlines on the front page declaring it was the 50th anniversary. The subprefecture government had kept its promise not to involve them in any celebrations or memorials after the 10th-year anniversary, so the date had crept up on them unexpectedly. The anniversary also meant they had been in service for over 75 years.

D974-T92 ignored the article and quickly flipped through the other pages of the paper. They stopped their superficial scanning when they came to the obituaries. After the massive cleanup of human bodies and biological matter the Haruki-Chikara robotic teams undertook in 2062, D974-T92 had become unusually sensitive to human death.

In fact, all the D974-Ts that were part of the Haruki-Chikara robotic teams had been affected. The months of gathering the dead of all ages for identification and cremation, and their pets and wild creatures for mass cremation, had caused many of the D974-Ts to malfunction.

A large percentage simply stopped moving once the work was done. Others developed idiosyncratic movements, like pacing in circles, that were reminiscent of zoo animals that developed psychotic patterns of behavior when isolated from their natural habitats.

Efforts were made to diagnose the D974-Ts, including classifying their symptoms as Haruki-Chikara syndrome. Nothing specific was identified as being abnormal in their programming or cybernetic brain functioning. But once the unusual behaviors began, there was no rehabilitation possible.

Robotic scientists had even collaborated with psychologists to intervene. Groups of D974-Ts were brought together in "group" sessions to share their Haruki-Chikara stories with the idea that they could process their experiences together. Unfortunately, these sessions led to the mass initiation of Haruki-Chikara syndrome for 99% of the participants.

It turned out that robots did not "process" and move past experiences like traumatized humans. They could not forget what they had experienced individually or what they heard. And sharing stories with other D974-Ts simply loaded more of the memories and imagery into their cybernetic brains, which seemed to trigger the symptoms.

Hundreds of D974-Ts were affected by Haruki-Chikara syndrome before researchers determined that reassigning them to reconstruction and recovery of the city's buildings and infrastructure could prevent, or at least delay, the onset. Tens of thousands were deployed in the city, while hundreds more were sent out to the asteroid belts to help with the mining operations.

D974-T92 re-read the obituary for a three-year-old girl a dozen times before they could make themselves stop. They hadn't seen a child since the Haruki-Chikara cleanup. Their fragile bodies had always seemed so small compared to the piles of debris and destroyed buildings. Akkeshi was a city slowly being repopulated by humans but was still considered a hazardous zone where no children were allowed to live because of the risks of radiation and chemical exposure.

As D974-T92 stood over the open pages, an unusual thing happened. Scores of nanites flowed off their fingers and into the paper they held in their grasp, exposing their metal digits. D974-T92 scanned the surrounding area to make sure no one had seen this "lapse" in their maintaining a human appearance, a violation of the Robotic Treaties which came with harsh penalties. They dropped the paper once they glanced down again, quickly sending additional nanites to re-cover their fingers.

Their nanites had interacted with the water and seeds in the paper to start the plants sprouting. In fact, the nanites were accelerating the growth process to the extent that within a minute the paper was converted into a pile of composted material with a small riot of flowers topping it.

D974-T92 quickly scooped up the pile of organic matter and rushed to the back of the plant and through the door to the outside. They threw open the lid of the disposal system and dumped the load in their hands into it. Slamming down the lid, they pushed the button to engage the system and waited until the noise of the cycle finished before reentering the building.

D974-T92 spent the rest of their shift folding and unfolding origami flowers, trying not to think about the ones they had destroyed in the disposal unit.

Part II.

That evening, when D974-T92 returned to their apartment, they could not appreciate the origami that covered the walls and decorated the ceiling. They hurried past the delicate artwork to enter their maintenance station, standing in front of the full-length mirrors as the nanites retracted the imitation human tissue and left the underlying metal exposed.

Stood staring at themselves for hours, unmoving.

At 9pm, the evening city-wide alarm sounded, and D974-T92 exited their apartment and made their way to the roof. All the other robots in the building would enter stasis to conserve energy, but D974-T92, the lone D974-T in the housing complex, would not.

The night was clear, and the stars were bright pinpricks of light across the sky. D974-T92 positioned themselves at the eastern edge of the roof and began their recitation. Although they could complete it within a few seconds if they chose simply to scroll through the written list of names, D974-T92 spoke the identification numbers of their fellow D974-Ts lost to Haruki-Chikara syndrome out loud, slowly, and respectfully. The spoken recitation took them most of the night.

As they came to the last name, D974-T92 began reaching out to the other D974-Ts still in the city. Although they could not access the D974-Ts mining in the meteorite belt, they could connect with the thousands of D974-Ts remaining in the city.

Here, they allowed themselves the full advantage of their processing and communication speeds to meet with each D974-T, each sharing an innocuous aspect of their day. The D974-Ts had discovered that this ritual sharing of minor daily events was a potent factor in postponing Haruki-Chikara syndrome.

D974-T92 was careful to avoid sharing anything about the 50th anniversary, the girl's obituary, or especially the episode with the flowers. They were not convinced that they were not seeing the beginnings of Haruki-Chikara syndrome in themselves and were cautious of contaminating the others with these incidents.

As dawn broke over the city, D974-T92 ended their connection to the other D974-Ts and headed back to their apartment. They spent a short time in the maintenance station to fully recharge from the night's expenditures, then reestablished their fake human "skin" and headed back to work.

Part III.

The day was uneventful, and D974-T92 passed by the rear door of the plant repeatedly, as they avoided touching any of the newspapers. After the six dozenth approach, D974-T92 exited the building. They went to the disposal unit, futilely opening the lid to examine the interior, knowing that there would be nothing left of the flowers.

After setting the lid back into place, D974-T92's attention was caught by a piece of paper blown by the wind. The paper passed down the alley and was caught at the corner of the building. As the trapped paper shifted with the breeze, a flash of pale yellow was revealed and then hidden beneath it.

D974-T92 made their way down to the stuck paper and bent to lift it from the ground. Underneath was a faded flower from the seeds that had sprouted yesterday. It must have dropped to the ground as they were carrying the plants to the disposal unit. D974-T92 reached down to pick up the limp flower by the stem and their nanites once again flowed from their fingers to rouse the flower to uncurl its petals.

D974-T92 heard a gasp to their right and turned to see an old man leaning on a rake in a small open space between the buildings. The man's face was heavily wrinkled, and he stood slightly hunched over the rake, but his eyes were sharp as they stared at the revived flower in D974-T92's hand. D974-T92 quick scan of the area revealed only the lone man and small bunches of flowers and vegetables spotting the small space where the man stood.

It had been many years since D974-T92 had interacted directly with a live human. They did not seek out human company, and the city was still so sparsely populated after the clean-up that it was rare to run into a human during their daily routine. They and the man stared at each other in silence for a few moments before the man spoke.

"I wish I had as green a thumb as you do, Robot San," the man said in a soft but surprisingly strong voice, a grin spreading across his face. D974-T92 processed the man's facial expression and determined that the man's intention was to be friendly and that the statement was meant to be humorous.

"My name is Midori Tatsu. I was the Master Gardener of Kumamoto. I retired here in 2100 hoping to make a difference in the city after the Haruki-Chikara cleanup. But I've done little to live up to my reputation."

His right arm gestured, sweeping to encompass the small struggling garden. "There aren't many open spaces to begin with, and the soil is very poor."

At the man's beckoning, D974-T92 slowly approached the edge of the green space to stand in front of him. "Do you speak?" the man asked.

"I am designed to communicate using human speech," D974-T92 responded.

Tatsu laughed. "Yes, I hear that."

After a moment of silent appraisal, Tatsu said, "I recognize you. You are a D974-T model, right? The ones that did the cleanup?"

"Affirmative. Our identification is D974-T92."

Tatsu's eyes widened, and he straightened. "*The* D974-T*92*? The hero of the Haruki-Chikara disasters?!"

"Affirmative."

Tatsu performed a deep bow, his hands in namaste. "It is through your and the other D974-Ts efforts that I have any hope of making this small plot of land thrive again. Let alone fulfilling my dream of making the entire city green again."

D974-T92 stood silently, waiting for Tatsu to continue.

"Do you think your green thumb would work on live plants, Robot San?" Tatsu asked.

"D974-T92 does not have enough data to answer this question. D974-T92 has not attempted to do the same for live plants. We only have evidence from the green paper and this sole flower." D974-T92 held the flower out to Tatsu.

Tatsu gently slipped the flower from D974-T92's fingers. "Green paper, huh? I thought I saw you putting something into the disposal yesterday. What was that?"

"D974-T92's nanites activated the seeds in the green paper without an explicit directive. D974-T92 determined it was optimal to dispose of the flowers that were an indication of a malfunction."

Tatsu's eyes narrowed. "A malfunction? Ah, you think it might be a sign of Haruki-Chikara syndrome."

"It is a distinct possibility that D974-T92's idiosyncratic behavior is because of Haruki-Chikara Syndrome."

"It's been 50 years since the disasters. Surely you would have developed Haruki-Chikara Syndrome before now, right?"

"The probability decreases every year past the disasters, but there is no conclusive evidence that the probability drops to zero. It is impossible to prove an absence."

Tatsu considered D974-T92 as he twirled the flower in his hand. "I don't think this 'glitch' is a sign of Haruki-Chikara syndrome, Robot San. I think it could actually be a very powerful gift."

"A gift?"

"Robot San, the work you and the other D974-Ts did was something next to miraculous. But the initial efforts were put into the cleanup and disposal of the dead and the destroyed. It wasn't until Haruki-Chikara Syndrome was identified as a pandemic among the D974-Ts that you were tasked with salvaging and rebuilding.

"It's theorized that the work of putting things back together, of creating a city out of rubble, was what helped the D974-Ts avoid Haruki-Chikara syndrome. And what could be more creative and restoring than the ability to grow things?"

D974-T92's gaze shifted from Tatsu's face to the flower in his hand. They then raised their eyes to survey the struggling plants in the area behind Tatsu.

"How would you like to get more data?" Tatsu asked.

"More data would assist in determining if D974-T92 is malfunctioning."

"Then come into my garden and let's see what you can do with my plants."

Tatsu turned to lead D974-T92 to a patch of flowers that were struggling to grow in the loose soil.

"What do you advise D974-T92 to do?"

"Just do whatever you did before. Whatever comes naturally."

D974-T92 knelt down beside the flower bed and passed their hands over the tops of the flowers. Nothing happened with their nanites. The imitation skin remained firmly attached to their fingers.

"Try putting your hands in the soil," Tatsu suggested.

D974-T92 complied and sunk their hands up to the wrists in the slightly moist dirt. Within a few seconds, the nanites disappeared from their fingers into the soil beneath the plants. For a few moments, nothing happened, and then the flowers straightened and started to grow.

"Amazing!" Tatsu shouted as more and more flowers erupted from the dirt, filling the space with color and the air with fragrance.

D974-T92 continued to kneel on the ground as the effects of the nanites spread throughout the garden. Patches of sparse greenery soon were filled with flowering bushes, swaths of blooming flowers, and plants heavy with vegetables of all kinds.

The wood and metal shed at the back of the property slowly dissolved in on itself as the nanites claimed the carbon and other chemicals needed to do their work. Tatsu jumped and then barked a laugh when the rake he was holding dissolved from his hands into the ground beneath his feet, causing a vine of deep rich green to spiral around his leg.

"This is the miracle I was hoping for! Look what your gift is capable of!" Tatsu carefully unwound the vine to free his leg and scampered excitedly around the garden from one heavy growth to another.

From their position on the ground, D974-T92 turned slowly to examine every square inch of the gardens. This was something they would share with the other D974-Ts tonight, each of the D974-Ts.

Epilogue (Year: 2122)

D974-T92 laid their hand on top of the tombstone at the peak of the hill in the center of the park. The inscription on the tombstone read: "*Midori Tatsu, 2023- 2120. Master Gardener and the visionary of the ReGreen Akkeshi project. The Green Dragon who brought the spirit of Akkeshi back to life.*"

D974-T92's gaze wandered across the landscape they, Tatsu, and the other D974-Ts had created together. In the eight years between their first accidental meeting and Tatsu's death, D974-T92 and Tatsu had designed and carried out a plan to revitalize the city by bringing back nature. Tatsu's credentials as a Master Gardener gave him the clout to push through a city-wide program utilizing the D974-Ts. They pulled the D974-Ts from whatever service they were assigned and brought them under the supervision of D974-T92, with ultimate authority for the project lying with Tatsu.

In the months it took Tatsu to develop and win approval for the *ReGreen Akkeshi* project, D974-T92 experimented with their nanites to fully understand what they were doing to make the plants bloom. Released from their job at the newspaper, they could spend up to 20 hours a day investigating and perfecting the processes the nanites used. Tatsu partnered with them to explore growing plants native to the region that could thrive with only general horticultural maintenance by D974-Ts in the future.

During the first year of the project, D974-T92 worked to instruct the other D974-Ts on how to direct their nanites to replicate the capability of D974-T92's "green digits", as Tatsu affectionately called them. Tatsu's plan included using the unclaimed biological material from the residents, pets, and wildlife victims of the tsunami as the raw materials for creating this and the other parks and green spaces throughout the city. The massive loss of human and animal lives was transformed into a source of new life.

Over the years, the D974-Ts moved sector by sector through the city, working their magic of regeneration. For Tatsu, the *ReGreen Akkeshi* project was the ultimate expression of the years of dedication he had made to his craft and was the culmination of his life's work. Beautifully designed gardens, parks, and green spaces with water features were placed around the city until it seemed that every bit of free space turned colorful with life.

After the first few years of work on the *ReGreen Akkeshi*, D974-T92 came to a startling realization—there were no new incidents of Haruki-Chikara Syndrome happening in the D974-Ts. The work they had done in the initial clean-up after Haruki-Chikara disasters had eroded the psychological stability of the D974-Ts. But the work they were doing now to re-green the city was having a stabilizing effect.

Tatsu suggested that D974-T92 bring the D974-Ts affected by Haruki-Chikara Syndrome to the work locations and encouraged D974-T92 to engage with them several hours a day to incorporate them into the work. It began slowly, with the D974-Ts sitting in the developing gardens as the work progressed around them. Then D974-T92 moved to having them place their hands in the soil and interact with the plants. And D974-T92 recruited the other D974-Ts to share their experiences like they had done each night for years, one-on-one, but now it was sharing as a group.

The patience and effort eventually paid off as the Haruki-Chikara Syndrome D974-Ts began to help with basic labor of digging and moving materials, moving on to learning how to grow plants like the other D974-Ts. The work they did to resurrect nature in the city rehabilitated most of the D974-Ts that everyone thought lost to Haruki-Chikara syndrome. Now, D974-T92's recitation list was down to a handful of D974-Ts who remained catatonic.

ReGreen Akkeshi finished four months before Tatsu's death. He celebrated the success of the project's completion, then enjoyed his last days sitting in the shade of a tree in his favorite park, creating a plan to take the work of the D974-Ts to disaster sites around the globe. Due to his unceasing dedication, their first international project was starting the following spring.

D974-T92 bent to sink their fingers into the soil in front of the tombstone. Fresh flowers sprouted to cover the grave and brush up against the tombstone. They rose and walked down the hill to inspect the work of a group of D974-T92s at the west end of the park.

D974-T92 missed Tatsu's boundless enthusiasm and energy. But something new had come to the city. The sound of children's laughter.

Odd Behaviors

by Ian Ehrhart (Honorable Mention)

"Do you know what AB is?" Principal Baxter asks.

The interviewee puts on a confident smile and nods. "Absolutely!" he says with a bit too much enthusiasm. He actually doesn't know what AB is aside from the article he skimmed through as he was applying online. He can't even remember what the acronym stands for and believes 'AB' stood for 'Altered Behavior'. All he remembers is that it's where the more disruptive students are sent and that it pays more than General Education. Life Skills also paid more than Gen Ed, but he is scared about handling children with debilitating disabilities.

Principal Baxter looks down at his resume and fights to sustain her warm smile. He has an impressive resume, but for an administration role. What stands out as strange to her is that this is a massive leap from the corporate world to an elementary school. He has only one reference for an alleged tutoring job that seems so hastily written that she would bet it was his mother's number. She would have won that bet.

She shuffles her papers around and continues the interview. "The Adaptive Behavior program is part of the Special Education Department for children who have difficulties regulating their emotions and behaviors. How would you, as a paraprofessional, handle a child that's going through a crisis because they don't want to do their assignment?"

He ponders for a moment, recalling all the times he's ever watched a school-themed sitcom. He doesn't remember any of them having a special education episode, so he does his best. "I would calmly talk with the student and do my best to relate to them to deescalate the situation." Instead of stopping with his satisfactory answer, he decides to keep going. "From my experience, giving them different or harder work helps as well.

Sometimes a kid is just acting out because what they're doing is too easy for them." He would later kick himself for saying this.

He feels a shift in the interview and knows that he butchered his chances. She has this pitying smile every other interviewer has given him when they already made their decision. He finishes the rest of the interview answering basic questions about his previous jobs, but he knows she is phoning it in. He shakes her hand, and she promises to let him know soon if he gets the job. He returns to his car, which has been cooking under the hot sun and lays back in his scorching leather seat for almost an hour before going home. He lies to his wife that everything went well, and that he believes that he'll get the job. Late at night, with his wife sleeping soundly beside him, he stays up all night looking at an empty inbox with a growing pit in his stomach.

The following Thursday, he is preparing to do an interview at another grocery store and dreading having to once again compete with children and the elderly for minimum wage. His phone buzzes as he's heading out the door, and when he answers, it's Principal Baxter. He drops to his knees and silently thanks God as the principal informs him he got the job and that he starts after the holidays.

He arrives twenty minutes early to Doe Elementary and parks in the visitor area. He spent the entire Christmas break going through copious amounts of paperwork and appointments to finally be an elementary school paraprofessional. He has never done a job like this before, and his nerves are on edge.

Since graduating from high school ten years ago, every job he has done has either been manual labor or desk work. He begins to doubt if this is the right job for him and maybe he should quit. He then remembers that no one else has reached out to him for any of the other jobs he applied for and that the bills are piling up. His wife is paying for most of them, but he can't keep using his credit card. He takes a deep breath and compromises that he'll quit the second a better job lines up for him. As he gets out of his car and walks towards the entrance of the school, his worries about the job seem to fade. He believes that if he can handle grown men and women in the workplace, he can handle some children. He had already forgotten the program he had signed up for.

After receiving his temporary substitute badge and wandering into the wrong hallways, he finds the AB classrooms on the opposite side of the school, away from the gen ed population. Before the students arrive, he introduces himself to his new coworkers. The teachers in the classrooms were Mr. Eddard, math and science; and Mr. Osweiler, reading and social studies. There are also two other paraprofessionals, Ms. Drew and Ms. Springer. They all have backgrounds in education and have been working in schools for over ten years.

Ms. Drew speaks with a strong New York accent and is an experienced paraprofessional who is working her way up to administration. Mrs. Springer is working on her master's degree in education to become a college professor. Unlike Ms. Drew, Mr. Osweiler has a thick southern accent and is also a football coach on the side. Mr. Eddard is a veteran and has been a teacher for almost five years, but this is his first time teaching special education.

As Mr. Osweiler and Mr. Eddard are discussing their lesson plan for the day, Ms. Drew and Mrs. Springer show the new guy what he would be doing every morning. The students in AB each have a goal sheet that shows how many points they made. If a student exhibits negative behavior, like not raising their hands or throwing objects, they would get an 'R', a reminder, instead of a point. All the new guy has to do is calculate each student's total points from yesterday and input them into the system.

Determined not to make a mistake on his first day, he thoroughly analyzes each scoresheet to be as accurate as possible. Data entry work has always made sense to him. Simple, mundane tasks were his preferred assignment, and he always excelled at doing the work no one else wanted to do. He is so engrossed in the multitude of spreadsheets that he doesn't even hear the first few students walking in.

He looks up from his computer to see why everyone is talking and sees a little boy mere inches away from his face.

"You're not Ms. Dante," says the boy.

The new hire looks around and realizes that he's surrounded by several curious children. They all ask the same questions of him and of each other.

Before the stranger can answer, the boy immediately coughs in the man's face and wipes his snot-covered nose with his bare arm. The other children bombard him with personal questions, some grabbing onto his shirt and pulling him around.

Mr. Osweiler uses his booming voice to quiet the classroom. "Ms. Dante moved to the front office. You guys don't need to worry about her, and you'll probably see her walking through the halls. She's going to be all right."

Mr. Eddard chimes in as well. "I know you guys loved Ms. Dante, but she has a new job to do." He gestures towards the new hire, who is desperately wiping spit that was coughed onto him off his face. "Why don't you introduce yourself?"

Before he can, a first-grade girl raises her hand. "Are you a new teacher?"

The man shakes his head with a smile. "No, I'm the new para."

A second-grade boy jumps up and down in his seat. "Your name is Mr. Para?"

Mr. Para tries to correct the kids, but it is too late. The children have already cemented in their brains that his name is Mr. Para. His coworkers do their best to hide their laughter but fail. The students quickly lose interest in Mr. Para and instead bring up the subject of breakfast and what is on the menu.

As Ms. Drew and Mrs. Springer wrangle the kids, Mr. Eddard leans in to whisper, "I wouldn't worry too much what the kids call you. They'll forget your name a hundred times before they finally have it down. You have to keep hammering it into them until they get it right."

The children, however, never forgot and refused to call him anything other than Mr. Para. It became such a popular joke that even the other teachers and staff began to call him that name too. The day he heard Principal Baxter utter his nickname; Mr. Para finally resigned all hope. He would forever be known as Mr. Para.

While on the job, he learns that the children in AB are all mixed grades and are given a mixed education. Mr. Eddard and Mr. Osweiler adjust the level of math, science, reading and social studies the children learn each day. There are seven children in total in the classroom: Nina–first grade, Charlie–first grade, Hugo–second grade, Vincent–second grade, Paula–third grade, Chester–fourth grade, and Benny–fifth grade. All the students stay together until first recess, where they're split into two groups. Ms. Drew takes all the students in first through third grades, while Mrs. Springer takes the fourth and fifth graders. Mr. Para's job was to float between classrooms and help when needed.

His first week ran smoothly as he got to know the other students. Nina and Hugo are best friends, and they need to sit next to each other. Charlie likes to play with Vincent and Benny, but not with Nina. Chester will opt to play by himself or be on his computer rather than socialize with the others, unless it's Benny, but only in small bursts. Benny plays with anyone and everyone who would listen to him talk.

Mr. Para didn't understand why these kids were even in this program. It seemed easier than the general education classes, and the students in AB acted like any other child would. Every kid he's ever met had issues of work avoidance or lashing out because they wanted to keep playing. Mr. Para was guilty of doing these things when he was a child, but he wouldn't have put his younger self into special education for it. None of this made any sense until the start of his second week.

Mrs. Springer is out for the day because of a doctor's appointment that she had already warned them about last week. Mr. Para offers to help Ms. Drew escort the littles to recess while Mr. Eddard keeps the other two in his classroom.

Barely a second after leaving the classroom, Nina steps out of line to walk with Mr. Para. He turns to Ms. Drew for direction, and she gives him a look to handle this. He nods and speaks with the sweetest tone he could muster. "Sorry, Nina, but can you please get back in line with everyone else?"

"No!" Nina says defiantly. "I don't want to walk with them! I don't want to be in the back! Vincent is walking too slow!"

Mr. Para remains firm. "Everyone else is in line, so you have to too. We're almost to the playground, and when we're there, you don't have to be in line anymore!"

Nina is adamant that she will not get back in line. He looks to Ms. Drew again for help, and she taps on the folders she's holding that has all of their goal sheets for the day. Mr. Para hasn't written anyone a reminder yet and has been too nervous to do so. He knows that Band-Aid has to be ripped off; he just hates that it has to be today.

He looks down at Nina, who is crying and begging to stay out of line. Other teachers in the hall are looking at him, and he can't help but feel judged that he can't handle the student. "Nina, if you don't get back in line, I'm going to have to write you a reminder."

Nina cries even harder, practically screaming at him not to give her a reminder and to let her walk with him. "I'm sorry, Nina, but you're getting a reminder."

It is almost like a switch was flipped and a signal sent to all the children in AB. Nina stops crying on a dime and turns to Hugo, who is watching her have a meltdown. Nina rushes towards him and shoves him into a wall. As Hugo is crying on the floor, the other students slowly shuffle themselves away from Nina, whose rampage is getting worse.

Ms. Drew sighs and gives her folders to Paula, who is leading the line. Ms. Drew grabs Nina by her shoulders and looks to a nearby teacher watching the chaos unfold. "Go get some AP's please." She tells them.

The teacher nods and hurries to the assistant principal's office.

Sweet Nina, the first grader who drew him a picture and always wanted to hold his hand, is no longer lucid. She is in a whole other plane of existence, growling, cussing, and kicking as if her life depended on it.

Mr. Para is stunned and wants to do something, anything to help. "What do I do?" he asks Ms. Drew desperately. He is scared out of his wits and sends himself down a spiral of self-targeting, believing that it was his fault Nina is like this.

Ms. Drew mutters something under her breath. "Not much you can do until you're CPI certified. Make sure the other kids are quiet and still in line."

Mr. Para feels useless. He takes the folders from Paula and sees his students are jealously watching the other children playing outside. They couldn't care less about Nina's tantrum; all they want to do is go to recess.

Two APs quickly make their way to help Ms. Drew, with Mr. Eddard close behind them.

"Mr. Para," says Mr. Eddard. "Can you please go help Ms. Drew and the APs take Nina back to the classroom? I got the kids from here."

Mr. Para nods and follows as the APs drag Nina back to Mr. Eddard's classroom. They take her to a corner of the room where there is a pink square called a zone. The walls surrounding that corner are damaged and look as if the school has plastered and re-plastered the same wall over and over again.

Nina knows where they're taking her, and she tries everything in her power to stop them. She flips over desks and chairs with only her feet and even manages to do a backflip off one of the AP's knees to kick Mr. Para in the face, all the while she's grinning from ear to ear. It is quite possibly the worst way for Mr. Para to find out that she took extensive ballet classes.

Mr. Para watches in silence as the APs and Ms. Drew restrain her, talk her down, and then finally let her go so that she can sit in silence. Nina has a blank expression on her face, as if she were a doll. The APs sit near her in case she acts up again.

Ms. Drew stands by Mr. Para. "Looks like the honeymoon phase is over," she whispers.

"What do you mean?"

"The honeymoon phase." She repeats herself as if he should know. "It's over, done. It's what happened to the last girl before you. First couple weeks were fine, but then something like this goes down," she gestures to Nina. "Now all the kids know that you know what's expected."

After about twenty minutes of trying to get Nina to speak, she finally does and it's as if nothing happened. She apologizes for everything she did and even draws another picture for Mr. Para to hang on his fridge. Mr. Osweiler peeks his head out from his classroom to see Nina being escorted to the cafeteria to have lunch, and he sighs. "I guess the honeymoon phase is done. It was nice while it lasted."

The day finishes uneventfully after Nina's meltdown. Mr. Para goes home and, instead of going to bed with his wife, he stays up all night going through his phone for job opportunities. After applying to over a hundred jobs in a night, he goes back to sleep hoping that one of them, any of them, will respond to his application. None do.

The very next day, Mr. Para shows up to work half awake, tired from staying up all night looking for jobs. He sits at the U-table in the back of the classroom and opens up his laptop to get started on his daily student data entry.

Mr. Eddard and Osweiler are stunned to see him.

"You're back? Even after Nina?" Mr. Eddard jokes.

He looks up from his computer, fighting the urge to close his eyes. "That's right. Those kids are stuck with me." This is only half true. What he really wants to say is that those kids are stuck with him until he gets a better job offer.

Mr. Para hopes that this is only a rough patch he's going through and that someone will eventually give him a call. However, after the days turn to weeks, and weeks turn to a month, Mr. Para finally realizes that he might be doing this for a long time. He then gives himself a new goal to just hold out until the summer.

Each passing day, the students find new ways to make his life hard. Nina and Hugo get riled up when voices get too loud. Charlie likes to use Benny to manipulate Vincent to get his toys. Benny hates doing his assignments and throws a tantrum whenever he is forced to do work. Each of them is on a hair trigger that could go off at a moment's notice. Despite all of their faults and odd behaviors, they all pale in comparison to the most difficult student in the class: Chester.

Chester exhibits all their problems and more. He only likes doing work that he already knows how to do. Chester hates girls in general and needs to be kept away from them. He refuses to participate in art, music, and PE. He purposefully isolates himself from the students in his grade because he would rather have conversations with himself. If anyone interrupts any of his daily rituals, he becomes violent towards himself, the environment, and anyone in arm's reach.

What makes things worse is that it is hard to stay mad at these students. He has seen from firsthand experience that they are not in control when they go into crisis. The teachers and paras try their best to redirect a student in hopes that they stay out of a negative mindset. The second the kids are lucid again; it is as if they have woken up from a dream. They apologize and return to being normal students until they inevitably go back into crisis because it's hard to regulate their emotions.

Another issue that Mr. Para has with the job is that he doesn't feel confident about himself. He is jealous of his coworkers, who are much better at this than he is.

All the students love Ms. Drew and always ask for her, sometimes even going into crisis if they don't get her attention. Mr. Eddard does impressions of cartoon characters that make all the kids laugh and is good at steering their attention away from what makes them upset. Mr. Osweiler carries himself with an air of authority and has the voice of an army drill instructor that makes the students think twice about whether what they're about to do is worth it. Mrs. Springer has a reputation for freely handing out reminders, which causes the kids to fix their actions quickly.

Mr. Para feels more like a fly on the wall, and that infuriates him; nothing makes him angrier than feeling useless. He is nearly perfect with his data entry submissions, but that's only a small part of the job. When he started, he felt above this kind of work, and now he doesn't feel worthy enough to be in the classroom.

He is soon forced into being hands-on the day Mrs. Springer turns in her resignation.

She has had enough of AB. The constant death threats, insults, and cussing is too much for her. On her last day, after school ends, she stops Mr. Para as he is heading towards his car. "You have to watch yourself with these kids." She warns him. "They say they're going to hurt you, and I believe some of them might. I've been stabbed, bitten, and cut by all of them. If I were you, I'd transfer and get a job in gen ed. Good luck, honey." She pats his cheek and saunters off to her car.

Mr. Para never sees her again.

With Mrs. Springer gone, Mr. Para is told that he would take the lead with their resident fourth and fifth graders. As the littles are lining up to go to recess, Benny and Chester are going to Mr. Osweiler's room. During the time when Mr. Para floated in between classes, he noticed that so long as Benny and Chester were together, they evened each other out. It is as if they didn't want to embarrass themselves in front of the other. Little did Mr. Para know that their symbiotic relationship would not last.

On his first day as lead para for the big kids, he is told that Benny had scored enough points to go back to the general education classes. He would only need to check in with AB in the morning before he could walk to his first class. Mr. Para is happy that Benny is moving up but is dreading the thought of Chester without a peer. Chester didn't seem to mind that Benny wasn't attending lessons with him anymore, but there is a shift in his behavior. He is faster to lash out, and all his other behaviors had been cranked up to eleven.

Every day becomes harder for Mr. Para, and he starts to forget his name. It takes his wife six times to get his attention because he's forgotten what it's like to be called by his proper name. He doesn't want to do this anymore. He wants out, but no other company wants to hire him.

"Is everything ok?" Mrs. Para asks.

Mr. Para hasn't told her anything about his job. He is embarrassed to tell her how things are actually going at work. He wants her to believe that he has everything under control and that he is a natural-born paraprofessional. She listens patiently to him and holds his hand.

When he is done, Mrs. Para smiles at him. "What you're going through sounds really hard. I couldn't imagine doing that. I think you should take advantage of the one-on-one time you have with Chester. Get to know him better, and you'll have a better chance of redirecting him."

The next day, Mr. Para does exactly as his wife suggested. Instead of standing at a distance during lunch, he sits at Chester's table, a couple of seats down from him. When Chester talks to himself, Mr. Para pretends that Chester is talking to him and answers, adding to the one-sided conversation. Every morning, Mr. Para asks Chester what he brought for lunch, and Chester is more than happy to tell him. Despite the progress Mr. Para is making in bonding with Chester, he feels like it isn't enough.

When it is time for PE, the coach comes up to him and says, "You're the new para for AB, right? Do you think you could get Chester to participate more? Mrs. Springer always pulled him aside and let him sit in a corner all last semester. He really needs to do his exercises."

"I'll try my best," he promises. Is it a sign from the universe? Mr. Para makes a new goal for himself: get Chester to participate. It is an uphill battle, to say the least. Chester refuses to show any type of enthusiasm for PE, music, or art. No matter how hard Mr. Para begs, bribes, and threatens, Chester will not join the rest of the students.

During another day of PE, Chester sits near the back doors to wait for the class period to end as he usually does. Mr. Para sees the coach and her para doing the exercises with the kids who mimic what they're doing.

Mr. Para groans and sets down his folders when he realizes he hasn't tried what they're doing yet. "Come on, Chester," he says. "We have to do jumping jacks."

Mr. Para does a set of jumping jacks and realizes how out of shape he is as a sharp pain digs into his side.

Chester looks up at Mr. Para confused, then towards the other kids in front, then back to Mr. Para. Chester hesitantly stands up and starts to imitate Mr. Para. From jumping jacks to pushups to jogging in place, Chester does it all. Mr. Para can't get him to play jump rope games with the other kids, but Chester does all the exercises, and that means the world to Mr. Para.

His strategy doesn't stop with PE as Mr. Para takes part with Chester for every large group class he has. Every day of every week, Mr. Para is either making music, drawing, or exercising to get Chester to do so as well. It took time, but eventually he is able to get Chester to participate without even asking. Chester sits where he's supposed to, does the activity, and even socializes with the other kids if he feels up to it. The best part about this new dynamic is that Chester's outbursts have dramatically dropped. He still has an episode every other week, but no longer once a day.

As Mr. Para and Chester sit in art class, Mr. Para receives an email. He leaves the table to check what it is and sees that it's a job offer from a company he applied to. They offer better pay, better insurance, a 401k, and he could customize his cubicle. All he needs to do is pass the interview. He looks up from his phone to see the worst thing that could happen: A kid spills their colored water all over Chester's drawing.

It is as if the world stops. Mr. Para is too far away to prevent Chester from attacking the other child. The students at the table hold their breath. The one who spilt the water is on the verge of crying and braces himself for the assault. Instead, Chester closes his eyes, takes a deep breath, cleans the mess, then grabs a new sheet of paper to start over. There is no swearing, no assault, no crying, no blaming, no crisis. He simply lets it go.

Mr. Para brags to anyone who would listen that Chester didn't assault someone. He feels like he could jump over the moon with how happy he is. During his lunch break, he calls his wife to let her know that Chester didn't fight someone, and she cheers loudly over the phone. When he gets home, all he can do is retell the situation in as much detail as possible.

When the weekend finally arrives, Mr. Para has nearly forgotten about the phone interview. When his phone rings and they introduce themselves, Mr. Para becomes nauseous with guilt, almost like he is doing something wrong. The interview goes extremely well, and the company tells him he is their best candidate. He will have to work the night shift, and he'll need to do extra assignments after hours, but they assure him the pay is worth it. All he has to do is say 'yes.'

Monday morning rolls around, and Mr. Para shows up to work with a document stuffed in his pocket that he printed out at home. Ms. Drew is setting up the new scoresheets in the children's folders while Mr. Eddard and Mr. Osweiler are chatting about the upcoming carnival.

Mr. Para opens his laptop to start on the scoresheets from Friday when Mr. Osweiler knocks on his table with Mr. Eddard standing beside him. "Hey, we got an email from the large group teachers. They said you're doing a great job. They're happy to see Chester getting back into the groove of things."

Mr. Para feels something swell in his chest that couldn't be put into words. He has to calm himself down before reaching into his pocket to pull out a list of college classes.

Mr. Para asks them the most important question of his life: "Can you guys tell me how I can become a teacher?"

IT TAKES A VILLAGE
by Tassie Kalas (Honorable Mention)

I wish I hadn't met my grandmother for the first time in a cemetery. I wish our first touch had been a warm embrace instead of my hand resting on her sun-warmed tombstone. Mostly, at the tender age of seventeen, I wish that someone had prepared me for the shock of seeing my own name staring back at me from her granite monument.

Growing up, I didn't know much about my father's side of the family tree. Never one to share his feelings, unless they related to the family business, my dad spoke little about his life in Greece before he came to America at the age of thirteen with his two older brothers.

Although we gathered bits and pieces over the years—how he journeyed on the last voyage of a ship that had seen better days, how he docked at Ellis Island with only the name of a relative in his pocket—it was almost as if his story didn't start until the second he stepped foot on American soil. I never questioned the years leading up to that momentous event. To me, my dad was strong and invincible, larger than life. It was almost impossible to imagine him as a child.

His youth was so far removed from me that he might have been a descendant of Zeus and Hera, for all I knew. Because my grandparents on his side had died before I was born, it never occurred to me that my dad had mortal parents—a father who came to America to make his fortune working on the railroads and died when my dad was four years old, and a mother, the woman I was named after, who was left to raise five children all alone.

"She was a saint. A real saint." My dad had the same response anytime my siblings and I stumbled across an old photo of his mother and pressed him about her. "Beautiful, too." He would swipe at one eye with the sleeve of his shirt and change the subject before we could ask him why the woman in the picture was dressed all in black, and why, although she died in her forties, she had the unsmiling, troubled face of someone much older.

It wasn't until I was in high school that we took our first family trip to Greece. My dad hadn't been back to the old country in thirty-five years and was eager to show us the place where he'd grown up. While my little brother and sister and I longed to stay on the pristine beach in Nafpaktos the entire time, eating cheesy tiropites by the inky blue Ionian Sea, my dad had loftier ideas for his children.

We were convinced that his fascination with ancient ruins was ruining our vacation. By day we explored old castles and fortresses and trudged through museums and monasteries, pausing only to eat at sidewalk cafes before the whole town shut down for mesimeris (two-hour naps). Night after night we met with long-lost relatives (some who appeared to be as antiquated as their surroundings) and feasted on feta and souvlaki while family members we'd never met chattered long into the night in a language we didn't understand.

On the last day of our trip, the five of us piled into an old Mercedes driven by a distant cousin, Nikos. Never one to seek full-time employment, he volunteered to drive us up to Ano Hora, the remote mountain village where my dad was born. The car lurched and reeled as he navigated us around and around, one hand on the steering wheel, the other waving a lit cigarette at the oncoming cars that played chicken with us.

"Are we there, yet?" We'd been driving for an hour when I was forced to crack open a window to get a breath of fresh air. I tried not to look down over the edge of the cliff as we careened up the narrow one-lane road. Clutching my stomach, I fought to hold down the pastitsio I'd enjoyed at my last meal.

"This is nothing!" my dad shouted from the front seat, his eyes glistening with anticipation. "See that trail?" He gestured towards an overgrown path that disappeared up the mountain. "Rain or shine, I walked all the way up and down every day, just to get water." He paused for emphasis. "*Barefoot.*"

By now, my younger sister was sweating, and our little brother's face was turning the shade of a dill pickle. Even my mom's *Cherries in the Snow*—coated lips seemed to purse tighter with every turn. Oblivious to our discomfort, my dad escorted us down memory lane as we dry-heaved up the hallowed hills.

"We didn't have toys, but we always had fun." He smiled at the memory. "We played with the billy goats. And we made up a game like baseball, but we'd hit sticks and watch them fly through the air—it's a wonder none of us lost an eye." He ignored my mother's gasp. "The sheep bladders were the best—a real treat! They blow up like rubber balls."

My siblings and I looked at each other in horror. I felt a twinge of shame as I thought about our closets full of Barbies and Hot Wheels and Raggedy Ann dolls purchased without question by our father, who grew up happily playing with animal entrails and bits of wood.

"That tiny cave? Over there?" He pointed to a small opening in the side of the rocky face of the mountain. "That's where we hid from the Germans." He chuckled as if reliving a favorite family moment. "My brothers and I would throw rocks at their tanks." Shaking his head, he grew more serious. "Our village held them off for months."

I forgot about my car sickness for a moment and marveled at the bravery my dad was forced to display at such a young age. He spoke of the Germans as if they were no more threatening than the tiny green toy soldiers my little brother collected on his bedside table.

"I have to pee," my sister whined. "How much longer?"

Ignoring her plea, my dad continued his Greek documentary as if he could see the scratchy black-and-white reel whirling in his head.

"Everyone was starving, but we were the lucky ones. My daddy went to America when he was young and worked on the railroad for 15 years. He returned to Greece a wealthy man. Married the most beautiful woman in the village—your grandmother!"

Intrigued, I sat up straighter and studied the rugged scenery as we meandered up the mountain. I imagined my grandparents living here as a young couple, falling in love despite the hardships around them, having a wedding, then babies, one after the other.

My dad shook his head. "But my daddy got sick right after my baby brother was born. Back then, there was no medicine to cure him."

My shoulders slumped as he continued.

"We lost everything during the war, but not the land he'd bought. It was enough to grow crops to feed the entire village." A look of pride spread across his face. "And Mama had her chickens." He cast his eyes toward the top of the mountain. "That's how we survived."

As we circled higher, we felt the air turn cooler and watched the trees grow greener and denser outside our windows. At long last, the car came to a sputtering stop in a small town clearing, and we stumbled over one another to escape the cramped confines.

"It looks like a fairytale!" I spun in a circle, taking in the majestic evergreen trees, the charming rustic stone homes sprinkled along the cobblestone street of this sleepy little village time had forgotten. "This is where you grew up?" For the first time, I pictured my dad as a little boy, running through the sunlit field, a menagerie of bunnies and goats and stray sheep bouncing after him.

He smiled and nodded and pointed to an overgrown path leading up a hill. "From here we have to walk. Wait until you see the view!"

I groaned. It was growing hot. The only view I was interested in seeing was of the sparkling blue sea from my chaise lounge on the beach.

My dad shepherded us up the hill like we were little lambs, pausing every so often to point out something only he felt was significant—a patch of oregano, wild and fragrant, crunching beneath our feet, the song of a red-breasted bird, the tip of a wooden cross peeking over the iron gate of a cemetery. "That's where my mama and daddy are," he announced, prompting our driver/cousin to make a hurried sign of the cross over his burly chest.

We followed him past a stretch of stone houses that led to a larger one at the top of the road. "There it is!" My dad stopped abruptly, shielding his eyes from the sun as he gazed at the home that he'd left thirty-five years before. Although tended to by a relative who made the trek up the mountain once a month, the green shuttered windows stared vacantly at us.

"It looks ... smaller than I remember." His expression flickered from wonder to sadness as he led us to the front porch of his childhood home. Searching in his pocket, he pulled out an iron key that looked like a remnant from the Trojan War. We held our breaths as he fitted it into the lock, turned the worn handle and eased open the door with a creak. He seemed to forget we were with him as his feet echoed across the wooden floor, his eyes taking in the plain walls, the white lace curtains draped over the windows.

Spotting a plaque hanging over the stone fireplace, he traced his fingers over the engraved letters. "Tsoukalas," he read aloud. "Our name in Greek." The sound of his voice let us know that although the house looked empty to us, to him, each and every room was bursting with memories.

I gravitated to a worn wooden chest in the corner of the room with a cracked, leather-bound book resting on its scratched surface. I slid my hand across the cover, wiped the dust off on the leg of my jeans, and peeked inside. A grim-looking group in a collection of sepia-toned photos stared up at me.

My dad walked up and peered over my shoulder. "That's our family." He recited their names one by one as he pointed a thick finger at each face. "That's my mama with my sister, Youla, my baby brother, Paul, and my older brothers, Frank, and Charlie." His finger hovered over his oldest brother. "You never met Charlie. Everyone loved him. Said he looked like James Dean. He...." His voice trailed off. "There was an accident."

Dad's face wrinkled into a map of emotions as he pondered over other photos, remembering cousins and uncles as he turned each page. The last picture in the book, of a grinning woman sitting on a small wooden stool with three speckled hens at her feet, made him pause and smile. "And that's Mama with her chickens." He gazed downward for a moment as if the memory pressed heavily on him, then snapped the book shut before we could ask any questions. "Let's go for a walk!"

We filed out of the house behind my dad and stopped to admire the view of the village from the shady porch, the peaks of the mountains in the distance, the sprinkling of red roofs nestled into the countryside. A shrill voice interrupted the serenity of the moment.

"Angelos! Angelos!"

We jumped in surprise as a tiny woman dressed all in black approached the house. Her shoulders were hunched as if she carried the weight of the world instead of a simple wicker basket on her arm. She used a wooden cane to maneuver up the uneven steps and burst into tears when she reached my dad. A stream of Greek words escaped her lips as she pinched him on both cheeks, kissed him, then pinched him again. Unsure if she was angry or happy, my siblings and I stepped back and watched.

Moments later, another old woman, also in black, appeared at the porch steps, this one carrying a loaf of bread peeking out from beneath a blue cloth. Behind her came a third, holding a hidden offering tucked inside her apron. The three gathered around my dad like little crows and cawed at him in loud voices. They hugged and hollered, their mini-reunion echoing through the mountaintops. My dad pulled my mother into the circle, and they hugged and hollered some more.

"Why are they all wearing black?" I asked Nikos.

Unfazed by the dramatic show on the stoop, Nikos shrugged and answered in broken English. "Because their husbands are dead. They are happy to see your father. They say it has been too long."

My dad called us over, and the women turned their attention to me and my brother and sister. They flew towards us in a frenzy, hugging and pinching us and exclaiming things we didn't understand.

"They are neighbors," Nikos shouted over the cacophony. "They knew your grandparents."

The one who had carried the basket looked up at me and gasped as if she'd seen a ghost. She took my hand in her wrinkled one, squeezed it and whispered my name in Greek. She touched my hair, and then my cheek, and spoke in a hushed voice. Leaning in closer, I strained to remember some of the Greek I'd learned as a little girl, picking out the few words I knew. Young. Girl. Grandmother. My name over and over in Greek. This time, I didn't need Nikos to translate. The message was loud and clear. I looked just like my grandmother.

I thought of the photos I'd seen of her, the long, dreary black skirt she wore, the strong, thick hands, her fierce expression, and mentally photoshopped my young, smiling face for hers. Not able to fathom how anyone could possibly think we looked alike; I smiled and nodded politely at the furrowed faces that stared up at me.

The women refused to leave until my dad promised we'd stop by each of their homes for homemade glyka. I glanced over at Nikos for translation, and he pantomimed gagging himself with his index finger. We waved goodbye to them from the porch until their tiny figures disappeared from sight. Then we gathered up their offerings—strawberries freshly picked from a garden, a crusty loaf of bread still warm from the oven, a hunk of salty feta, a dozen brown speckled eggs—loaded them into the basket and followed my dad down the lane.

"This is where I trapped birds." My dad pointed to a grassy field. Seeing the sad look on my little brother's face, he hurriedly explained. "I played with them and then let them go." He led us further down the hill and gestured towards a shallow valley. "This is where my mama would hide us when we heard the planes coming. You get used to the shooting after a while."

I studied the back of my dad's head as we followed him down the same paths he'd traveled as a young boy, and it occurred to me that I'd never have a complete picture of his childhood. Like the old photo album in his family home, all I'd get were snapshots of chosen memories, as strong as Grecian columns, polished over time, and meant to be shared with the world. As we walked, I couldn't help thinking about the ones still waiting to be excavated, memories like jagged bits and pieces of ancient ruins left buried beneath the rubble of time.

We approached the rusty gate of the village cemetery and stopped to rest under the shade of a massive chestnut tree. My mom made a picnic for us, tearing the bread and cheese into hunks while my dad pulled strawberries out of the basket and rinsed them in a tiny spring that flowed at our feet.

"There's no cleaner water than this." He cupped his hands and drank. "Cold, too. What else did they pack for us?"

I reached into the basket. "Just these eggs." I held one of them in the palm of my hand, feeling its smooth, warm shape.

My dad examined the spotted shell. "We used to have eggs just like these. Mama loved her chickens. They were our pets." He got a faraway look in his eyes. "The night before my brothers and I left for America, she killed two of them." He drew in a ragged breath. "She wanted us to have a good meal before we left. Before we left *her*." His shoulders quaked, and his eyes filled with tears. "We promised we'd return, but we never had the chance before she died. Too much work, too little time..." He shook his head, a pained look etched on his face. "She was a good mother. The best." He rose to his feet and headed towards the entrance of the cemetery.

For moments, the only sound was of my brother and sister nibbling on the crunchy crusts of homemade bread. I allowed the weight of my dad's words to sink in. His show of emotion shocked me more than if one of the towering marble statues at the Acropolis had cracked open, revealing a red, pulsing heart within. Instead of being frightened by this rare glimpse of his soft side, I felt empowered by it. I wanted to know more.

We gathered up the remains of our meal and scrambled to catch up to him as he passed through the heavy iron gate. The rough wicker of the basket scratched my arm with every step as I rushed ahead to join my dad, who was scanning the markers, his eyes squinting in the sun, searching for his parents.

"How did your father die?" I asked him as we ambled through the maze of memorials.

"Pneumonia."

I let that information sink in, then braved my next question. "And your mother?"

He stumbled over a root in the path and caught himself. "She died of a broken heart."

The quest continued until we ended up in the corner of the cemetery by a tiny Orthodox church. "There they are!" he announced.

We followed him to a pair of matching headstones lying side-by-side, glistening under the Grecian sun. My dad seemed to shrink in size as he stood between them and placed a palm on each monument. For a moment, I imagined him as an innocent young boy full of hopes and dreams, holding his parents' hands, his whole life before him.

Nikos nudged me. "Your Yaya's name was Tasia—same as yours—short for Anastasia." He nodded sagely and lit a cigarette. "In Greek, that means rebirth."

My dad turned back to us, brushing off his hands. "I should have brought some flowers." He put his arm around my mother and led us towards the exit.

Suddenly, I remembered the eggs still nestled in the basket I held. "Wait!" I ran up to my grandmother's grave and knelt down before it. With the tip of my index finger, I traced the familiar name etched on the stone. It was then I realized it would take more than one trip to Greece for me to know my grandmother, more than a collection of old photographs or fragments of my dad's faded memories. For me to understand the woman who had lived and died on this mountainside, it would take a village.

"To rebirth," I whispered. "To hope." With that, I pulled out an egg, as fragile as life itself, placed it at the foot of her tombstone, and bowed my head.

At that age, I didn't know where I was going, but after this trip, one thing was certain—I knew where I was from. Long after I returned home, I'd remember the lessons I learned from a woman I'd never met, a woman who'd survived war and financial ruin and unfathomable loss, a woman who gave her children the courage to search for a better life. Long after I graduated from high school and college, got married, and had children of my own, I'd remember my grandmother in Greece who was so much more than a name on a tombstone, but a strong, brave woman who passed down her resilient spirit to my father.

When I think of her, I'm reminded that even when we have nothing, we have something to give. When I think of her, she's wearing colors as vibrant as a Grecian sunset.

When I think of her, she's smiling.

Arman and Armageddon
by Kyle McKee (Honorable Mention)

A ripe peach sun peeked over the slumbering horizon. Orange beams and cherry rays glistened on the snow-capped mountains. Arman Khorshidi watched the sky and drank deep the peaceful memories of long-lost summers.

From the fiery empyrean, sinister winds carried an angel's chorus and mortal cries. Arman watched the source of the mourning wail as it fled the eternal sunrise. In the heavens, he saw Death, one of the four horsemen of the apocalypse, ride through the clouds on a horse as pale as a corpse's eye. Its taloned hooves rent clouds into crackles of lightning. The rider was cloaked in shadows that defiled the waking sun's gentle glow into trailing mists of ink. Behind the horse, miles-long chains flailed like a cat-o'-nine-tails. Thousands of living and screaming humans were impaled on the chains and consumed by fire. The air filled with the all too familiar stink of burning flesh and sulfur. Arman's body shook as the horseman flew overhead. The torturous cries felt like an axe being driven through his head and into his soul.

Arman fixed his eyes on a mountain pass. Bloody light poured over a dark figure meditating at its base; its arm raised in a symbol of solace. Even through the ear-splitting noise, he could faintly hear it call to him.

As the tortured cries fled to the west, Arman heard a groggy moan behind him.

"Uuuuggh, fuck that guy," said Zayah, his thirteen-year-old daughter. "Every morning it's the same shit."

"Watch your language! And how do you know it's a guy?"

Zayah sat up in her sleeping bag and looked at Arman through black tangled hair and red-lined eyes. "If it were a girl, they'd be riding side saddle...." She slumped back down to the floor, then raised her head to add, "And they wouldn't be such a dick."

He closed his eyes and sighed. "Hard to argue with that."

They sat in comfortable silence for a beat. Arman wanted to let Zayah sleep in late, but he couldn't contain himself. "We should cross the mountain pass today."

Zayah was a roller coaster of motion and emotion. "You mean it? We're ready? We're ready. Finally, we've been ready for, like, forever. We should celebrate. Let's eat the Cap'n Crunch for breakfast."

"Alright," Arman shrugged. "It might be the last Cap'n Crunch in the world." He walked to their food stash and pulled out a vacuum-sealed bag of cereal. "And it's ours, all ours! Muahahaha."

Zayah snatched the bag out of his hands. "Ugh, don't be lame."

She shook the golden pillows and rainbow balls of sugar into a bowl, dumped powdered milk onto it, then poured a canteen of water over the mess, before half-mixing them with a spoon and digging in.

Arman bit his tongue at the insanity and thoroughly mixed an eighth cup of powdered milk with one cup of water in the bowl, then he sprinkled one and a half cups of cereal into it.

Zayah gave him the stink eye over mouthfuls of clumpy Cap'n. "Ew, gross. Who puts milk in *before* the cereal?"

"It's the civilized way." Arman waved his spoon in her general direction. "This is chaos."

Zayah lifted the bowl to her mouth and chugged the rest of the milk. Then, she continued to eat her semi-moist cereal. "There are *crunch* berries in Cap'n *Crunch*. They are not *crunchy* if they get too soggy. It's the way Admiral Horatio Magellan Crunch intended them to be eaten."

"Isn't he a Cap'n?."

"He got a promotion. It takes a fleet of ships to distribute his cereal."

Arman smiled at that and spooned mushy crunch berries into his mouth.

"The factory that made Cap'n Crunch is over those mountains."

"Do you think it still works?"

Arman did not. "Probably."

"Do you think it's actually safe on the other side of the mountain?"

Arman did not. "Maybe."

Silence hung over them.

"Do you think Mom and Tara made it to the other side?"

Arman took a beat to absorb her question. He tried to look for an answer in Zayah's almond eyes, but they were fixed on the empty bowl in her lap. He studied her round face and button nose, boxed in sullen black curls. Arman couldn't help but think she looked exactly like Tara, her older sister, did when she was her age. He saw the best parts of Mona, her mother, in her. The ugliest parts of himself hated the constant reminder of their absence.

He thought of Mona's last words to them. "We'll be waiting for you over the mountain pass."

"Yeah, of course," said Arman.

Zayah didn't look up.

Arman swallowed a lump in his throat. It had been a hard four years since they started their journey to the pass based only on rumors of safety, and a harder two years since they were separated from Mona and Tara. But he believed they would make it, and so could Zayah and he.

Eventually, Arman asked. "Do *you ... think* they made it?"

"Yeah." Zayah looked up and smiled. "Yeah...fuck yeah."

"Language," said Arman. "Now, let's get dressed and double-check our bags."

They ate, packed, said goodbye to their temporary home, and journeyed toward the mountain pass into the quiet ruins of a dead suburb.

Slow and careful, they traveled between yards and through miles of suburban maze. Now, on a familiar path they had thoroughly surveyed, scouted, and scavenged over the last few months, they scurried across winding roads lined with hollow homes. They crawled over crabgrass and concrete drives filled with weedy shrubs that towered over dilapidated cars.

Arman hopped a fence, crawled beneath a hedge, and crouched in its shadow on a thick patch of dandelion weeds. Times like these made Arman feel like a rat trapped in the crumbling maze of humanity's hubris.

He watched Zayah scurry under a rusty truck and crouch behind its front wheel. Her heavy hiking bag barely squeezed beneath the vehicle with her. Zayah sniffed the air, looked down the nearby road, and then mouthed the words "Dog Mom" at Arman before she rummaged through her pack's side pouch. Arman didn't second-guess her and did the same just before the stink of rotten offal and cold ashes washed over him. They pulled bricks of charcoal out of their packs, rubbed them on their armpits, and popped the bricks into their mouths to hide their scent. They sat stark still and quiet as mice.

Roughly seven feet tall, the Dog Mom strutted down the center of the street on what looked like ostrich legs fused into red-bottom stilettos. Its bare human-like ass and breasts rocked back and forth in an equestrian manner. Its exposed skull had the stolen face of a woman stretched over it, giving the creature a rictus smile. Chimp-like arms daintily held the intestines of its "dogs" with French-tipped talons.

Arman's eyes followed the intestine leashes to the three sorry humans that had been captured by the monster. Each human's "leash" ended in an emaciated torso resembling a prized greyhound. Their eyes had been gouged out, and they crawled on all fours with their noses to the ground like bloodhounds searching for a scent. Their lips had been removed, giving them permanent snarls. Worst of all, each "dog" wore a single piece of clothing, a shirt, a boot, a hat, something that tied them to their former humanity.

Arman closed his eyes, took a slow breath in through his nose, and sighed through the lump of charcoal in his mouth. Somehow, he had grown bored of this nightmare. Survival had become rote. He asked himself why he kept doing this. Why go on living and risk becoming one of those hellish things? Was his life better living like a rat, scampering from bush to bush, nibbling on half-decade-old trash? He looked at Zayah. She diligently watched the Dog Mom pass, crouched and ready to spring into action. Arman got out of his head and did the same.

Once the creature was out of sight, Arman counted sixty heartbeats, then wordlessly, Zayah and he moved in tandem again. He signaled her to stay put and removed a box of salt from his bag. Zayah rolled her eyes, touched her thumbs together, and pushed forward, signaling to keep going. He gave her a look that said, "Don't fight me on this now" and poured a thin line of salt over half of the road. She glared and clucked her tongue before pouring her own box of salt over the other half of the road, a trap for the demon on the off chance it doubled back. He could feel her annoyance at his over-caution, and he was frustrated with her brashness. But these differences kept them alive, and it kept them together, so they suffered each other's annoyance, else they'd suffer each other's absence. On opposite ends of the road and without preamble, they each spat into their right hand and rubbed their palms into either end of the salt line, then moved on. Cover to cover. Empty house to empty house.

Hour after hour, they scurried through dichotomous worlds of rotten bones and sleepy homes. There were beautiful moments hidden at the end of times. Arman and Zayah made crowns of flowers from a long-overgrown garden. They danced and sang in two-part harmony to drown out the siren-like wail of a passing cacodemon. They found a tree with ripe peaches in someone's backyard and sat in its shade, ate its fruit, and watched the end of the world drift by. These precious few moments with his daughter centered him. It made life's insanity feel distant.

Just as Arman closed his eyes to let a cool breeze wash his worries away, Zayah pulled him down into the overgrown grass and stuffed a lump of charcoal into his mouth. He held back tears trying not to choke on the taste of ashes and the smell of decaying innards.

Moments later he saw the ghoulish smile and skeletal eyes of a Dog Mom bob above the rotted fence across the yard. Arman heard her dogs snort and bump at the old boards like truffle pigs. He felt Zayah coil; her hand inched toward her hiking bag, likely to grab their only bottle of human tears. He put his hand over hers to stop. She was being brash. It was better to hide and wait in moments like these.

The Dog Mom pulled her dogs away. The back of its partially exposed skull made him think of a bloody pearl bouncing along an old dock.

Sixty heartbeats later and their peaceful moment had washed away. Horrid reality came roaring back like a tidal wave. Silently and together, they let themselves be swept up in its stream toward the slow beating heart of the mountains.

Rose-tinted rays settled over the horizon as the sun grew weary of watching Arman and Zayah journey through neighborhoods. It took over half a day to travel a mere four miles through suburbia. They took shelter on the second story of a home and stared out of an arched window that overlooked a little field across the street.

As the sun sank, Arman watched butterflies flit about a little red wagon on the edge of the field. He wondered if its previous owner used to live in this house. He wondered how old they were. He wondered if they had made it over the mountains.

Beyond the field was an interstate entrance ramp. Eight lanes of ancient concrete and rebar led to a valley through the mountains. At the mouth of the glen, there was what appeared to be a statue embedded in the cliff face, large enough to be seen from miles away. Arman had studied the passage long enough to know it was another monster, another trap. From here, he could feel the beat of its call. A slow and heavy drum that summoned its mindless slaves, which they called The Pilgrims. Arman's mind struggled against the lumbering pull of the eldritch beast. He wanted to be away from its influence and back in their hidey-hole where the day began.

Worry crept into Arman's heart. He thought of Tara and Mona's raft being swept away as they tried to take a shortcut through the swamps and were caught in the current of a Maelstromopheles demon. Mona and Tara floated down their intended shortcut while Zayah and he blew off course to a much longer route. It felt like the memories of a raving madman, a jumble of nonsense words Arman used to explain how his family was torn apart. He feared the mountain pass was another trap that would take Zayah from him too.

His thoughts, for the millionth time, went back to Mona's last words to them. "We'll be waiting for you over the mountain pass."

Arman flinched out of his daze when Zayah spoke. She sat up and pointed toward the last glimmer of the setting sun. "The Pilgrims are here."

Against the closing crimson eye, silhouettes shuffled down the interstate in ones, then tens, then thousands. Mindless droves of emaciated humans shambled toward the creature that guarded the mountain pass, as they did every night.

"We should call them zombies," Zayah declared.

"What? No, the Pilgrims don't eat people, or bite and infect them."

"But they're all fuckin' ugghh," Zayah held her arms out in front of her like Frankenstein. "Zombie-y looking."

"Language. And calling them Pilgrims just feels better. Do you really want to walk through a crowd of zombies to sneak past that big stone monster thing? Or do you want to feel like you are in the Canterbury Tales?"

"Ew, nobody even knows what that is. It sounds boring."

Arman teetered his hand in a so-so motion. They sat staring out of the web-like window in comfortable silence. Arman leaned over and hugged Zayah.

She hugged him back and rested her head against his shoulder. "Let's go find Mom and Tara."

Arman smiled. "Let's get through these zombies."

They packed and waited for nightfall.

Sunset's ruby eye fell over the field of monarchs and bumblebees. They flitted through verdant stalks and nestled on patches of blue speedwell and wild violet. Was this his Bifröst? Had they finally made it out of the shit and through the belly of the beast? Were the peaks in the distance its great maw? After years, would his and Zayah's search finally be over?

Arman and Zayah crossed the field of sleeping rainbows as night fell and a vulture-eyed moon rose to bear its ugly gaze upon them. Arman felt as if they had stepped into the spotlight of a grand theatre. The stars above, two hundred billion trillion souls trapped in the void, watched them with bated breath.

Arman paused to double and triple check the shoulder straps, chest and waist buckles, and zipper locks on Zayah's hiking bag, then she did the same for him. They walked up the ramp and onto the interstate. It made Arman feel small. He held Zayah's hand at the top of the entrance. Together, they stepped into the press of shambling bodies. It was hard to make out details in the dark. A sea of sunken eyes fixed on the looming jaws of the mountain pass. Filthy clothes hung off of malnourished bones.

The long walk along the crowded concrete road reminded Arman of what it was like to leave a sporting event. It felt like a lifetime ago since

Arman had been in a crowd of people. It had been just him and his family for years, and only him and Zayah for years after that.

The pair lumbered for miles in the dark mass. Cool mountain air brought with it the stench of warm, unwashed bodies.

Arman staggered along, doing his best impression of a zombie, eyes fixed on the impossibly large creature embedded in the mountainside. Thousands of feet tall, it could easily be mistaken for a half-finished statue of Buddha carved into the cliff side. Its legs were crossed, two hands rested in its lap, a third hand raised with its palm facing out, its squid-like head closed its eyes as if it were meditating. It appeared to sit on an emerald throne of birch and beech trees. Blooming mountain laurels and magnolias embroidered its rocky tomb with delicate white and pink flowers. Normally, Arman would have thought of this lush mountain valley as beautiful, but this close to the creature, he couldn't ignore the terrifying impact of its breathing, hundreds of thousands of tons of undulating vegetation and stone.

WHUM

The slow and heavy rise and fall of its rock-entombed chest felt like waves in the ocean. The weight of its breathing made Arman's entire body feel like it was expanding and contracting. It pushed and pulled on the barriers of reality. He was flotsam bobbing along the inexorable current of this dark god.

WHUM

Zayah tugged on Arman's arm to get his attention and whispered. "Dog Mom." She let go of his hand and shoved a lump of coal into her mouth.

Arman did the same, as the stink of rotten offal and cold ashes hit him. He spared a glance over his shoulder. The Dog Mom stood a head taller than the average Pilgrim. Moonlight gleamed off of its stolen smile and bits of exposed skull. The dogs wormed their way through the crowd of Pilgrims like kids in a corn maze. Arman snatched a box of salt out of his bag and pulled Zayah to run. She held her ground and pulled away from him. Her eyes seemed to say, "Calm down," as she covertly took a box of salt and a bottle of human tears out of her bag. She tilted her head to the right, then left. Arman glanced down at the salt and tears, then gave her a nod.

WHUM

Eyes filled with moonlight and mouths full of ashes, Arman and Zayah walked in opposite directions perpendicular to the Pilgrims' path. He looked down the highway and saw a pale crown above the swale of slaves, Dog Mom's skull bobbing along the center of the road. Close, but plenty of time to finish the ritual and run.

WHUM

He focused on his line of salt; the more intact it was, the more powerful the ritual would be. He poured it thick. Zayah would say it was no time to be so fuckin' stingy. Miraculously, the horde of Pilgrims gingerly stepped over the salt instead of trampling on it like he feared.

WHUM

Arman looked at Zayah; she worked with quick and steady confidence. Halfway there. He picked up the pace and chanced a glance up at the Dog Mom. Its pearly crown and plastic smile froze and turned to Zayah. The creature and its thralls surged toward his daughter.

WHUM

Arman scrambled on all fours, a mad dash to finish the trap, haphazardly dumping salt across the street.

RUN

Arman spit out his charcoal and yelled. "Zayah! Zayah, run!" He dumped the rest of his salt onto the street, spit in his hand and rubbed it onto the pile.

RUN

"Hey!" Arman screamed and jumped up and down. "Hey dog bitch, over here!"

Three shrill howls, wracked with pain, responded. A scythe of a smile turned on him. The horde of Pilgrims in its way were mowed down like crops under a combine.

RUN

Arman ran. He pushed and clawed his way into the crush of shambling bodies. Arman fought to get away from the inhuman hounds at his heels. He pushed to be by Zayah and keep her safe. He struggled to move. The Pilgrims grabbed him. Dozens of filthy hands and bony fingers dug into his weak flesh. They piled on top of him, crushing, scraping, and grinding. It stank of dirt and decay. It was dark. He couldn't breathe. He tried to twist, thrash, and claw his way free. But he did not gain an inch.

STRUGGLE

Arman's captors flipped him over and held his arms and legs as if he was being drawn and quartered. A pallid moon looked down on him. They held him up, presenting him to the demonic hounds on a tarnished silver platter. The Dog Mom and her three dog thralls waited on the other side of the salt line. The master couldn't cross the barrier, but its dogs were still human enough to pass it and drag Arman over. He saw the promise of eternity and torture in the hollow eyes of the demon. He didn't want to become one of those eyeless hellhounds with his intestine wrapped around a monster's claws.

STRUGGLE

The Dog Mom loosened her grip on the leashes. The dogs stalked forward.

"No!" Arman yelled and kicked. "No, no, no!" He was held in place, crucified on a hellish altar of flesh. He had one last desperate plea. "Zayah, run!"

A bottle of twinkling sorrow fell from the sky and shattered at his feet. Zayah had thrown her bottle of human tears to save him. A puddle of sadness and broken glass shimmered with starlight on the pavement between him and the hellhounds. The dog creatures raised their noses to the moon and made a sound between howling and screaming. The Dog Mom pulled on their leashes, but they surged forward, mad with desire. Blood and shit poured from their eviscerated stomachs in their frenzy. They yanked the demon halfway over the magic-infused salt. The Dog Mom's head and torso burst into sulfurous flames. Its cries of pain were hauntingly human as it rolled on the concrete in a futile attempt to put out the infernal fire. The hounds lapped up the tears, unaware of the glass shards slicing through their tongues and throats. The horrid scene filled Arman with joy and relief. He turned his head enough to see Zayah on the other side of the road. A wave of Pilgrims crashed into her and dragged her into their fold.

Zayah cried out before she disappeared. "Daddy! Help!"

DESPAIR

Arman took a breath to yell just as he was buried in an avalanche of bodies. Cadaverous fingers dug into his eyes, fish hooked his mouth and nose, pulled his hair, and crushed his groin. He felt like he was being dragged to the bottom of a mass grave. Deeper into the pitch-black crush of bodies, he kicked, punched, and wormed to exhaustion. He felt his clothes being torn to ribbons. His shoes were ripped off. His body became slick with sweat and blood. Only the hiking bag strapped around his shoulders and buckled around his chest and waist remained intact. Finally, he came to a stop. He was hoisted into the air above the heads of the Pilgrims. Filthy fingers dug into his skull and forced his eyes open. Arman screamed.

Thousands of feet up, two enormous cephalopod eyes watched him. Its gaze had the gravity of a dying star, towering sclera the color of pandemonium, and rectangular pupils like portals into the madness beyond the universe. This was the eye of judgement, and at the bottom of his soul he felt unworthy.

"Zayah! Zayah, where are you?" Arman yelled. He tried to turn his head, but his eyes could not tear themselves from the mountainous god's assessment.

There was silence.

"Where's Zayah? What did you do with her?" asked Arman.

The silent judgement grew.

"What do you want from us?" Arman whispered.

The mountain heaved upward as the creature drew in a deep breath. A voice shook Arman's bones down to the marrow.

LOVE

Someone pushed their way through the crowd of Pilgrims and wrestled Arman away from their grasp.

A voice. "Dad!"

Another voice. "Arman!"

Tara and Mona.

They grabbed Arman's hands and ran him through the crowd. His body felt stiff and swollen. Every step felt like walking on pins and needles. Arman stared at his bare feet slapping on concrete, afraid to meet the Olympic eyes of the creature above. But he had to see his wife and daughter. Slowly, he looked up. The Pilgrims seemed to peel away from Mona and Tara like blooming flowers.

They burst through the crowd. The pass lay ahead. A long and open road wound itself up the mountain valley. The path disappeared into a starlit horizon. Arman staggered to a stop. His body hurt. Tears rolled down his face.

Tara pulled him on. "Dad, we have to keep moving." Her heart-shaped face looked older, the lines harder than he remembered. Her flowing curly hair had been cropped short and militant. But her eyes and button nose were still the same as her mother and sister.

Mona lifted his arm over her shoulder to help carry his weight. "Arman, we have to go." She hadn't changed. Her dark curly hair was tied into a tight bun. Her face still had the gentle curves he fell in love with. His gaze lingered on her soft, top-heavy lips and almond-shaped eyes. He was dazed by her beauty.

Tara yanked his other arm over her shoulders, and they marched him down the road.

Arman was overcome with vertigo. "We have to stop."

Tara and Mona spoke in unison.

"We have to keep going. We need to get out of here."

Arman tried to wiggle out of their hold. But they pulled him along, and he was so tired. He wanted to let them whisk him away. Why fight them? Hadn't he dreamt of this moment? To be embraced by his family again? To lean on their strength where he was weak, and he felt so weak at that moment.

"I just need a minute." He whimpered. He became deadweight in their arms, but they hoisted him up and dragged him so the tops of his feet skid across the concrete.

"We have to keep going, Arman," said Mona.

"We can't look back," said Tara

"Somethings wrong," he said.

"Everything is wrong, it's the end of the world Dad."

"Something's missing," he said.

"Yes dear, everyone and everything is missing," Mona grunted and heaved him up. "They're all dead, or demons, or zombies." She tilted her head back to the crowd of Pilgrims.

"Zombies ..." Arman muttered. "Where's Zayah?"

They continued to march him down the road. They had almost made it to the far edge of the mountainous god's body.

"Stop!"Arman stood his ground and yanked his arms out of their hold. "Where is she?" He shook his head and wiped the tears from his face. He heard a distant voice. "Daddy!"

Arman turned to it. He looked back at his wife and daughter. They urged him away.

"Daddy!" The voice was smaller now.

"We have to get Zayah," he said and pulled them back toward the horde of zombies.

"No, please, Arman," begged Mona. "Don't leave us again."

Tara's lip quivered. "We can't do it without you."

Tears flowed as freely as the wind from his haggard eyes. They couldn't possibly suggest leaving her behind.

"She's still back there. I heard her."

"Arman it was nothing, we have to get away from here." Mona gently took his hand.

"Dad," Tara's grip was firm. "Zayah's gone."

"No!" he yelled. "We have to go get her. We're not leaving your sister!" Arman pleaded and looked at Mona. "Your daughter."

They were eerily still, like mannequins wrapped in memories. This couldn't be Mona and Tara. This couldn't be real. They would never leave Zayah on purpose. This must be an illusion, a test, a trap, a curse. Even if his memories of Tara and Mona were just idyllic dreams of who they really were, this was not them. At least, that's what his breaking heart told him.

Arman took a step back. This time they did not try to stop him. "I love you. I'll never stop looking for you," he said through heavy tears. "Zayah and I will meet you on the other side."

Mona looked at him with pity. "You won't make it out alone."

"I..." he choked back a sob. "I miss you. Wait for me!" He ran back into the swarm before he could change his mind.

This distant sound of Mona's voice being swept away in a maelstrom echoed in his head. "We'll be waiting for you over the mountain pass."

Arman barreled into the mob. "Zayah! Zayah!" He cried out again and again. A mantra, a prayer, a plea.

DESPAIR

Deeper and deeper, he burrowed into the maze of macilent masses. He became lost in the dark tangle of limbs. Vacant eyes all around him stared slack-jawed at the horrid god enshrined in the mountain. Arman pushed his way back and forth through the crowd. Half blind and mad, yelling himself hoarse, unable to look up in fear of meeting the eye of divinity.

DESPAIR

Someone crashed through the crowd of slaves and took Arman by the hand.

A voice. "Daddy!"

"Zayah!"

Rivers of tears shimmered down her face. "I saw Mom and Tara. They wanted to leave you. And I just, I..."

Arman hugged her. "It wasn't real. I saw them too. It wasn't real." He told himself as much as her. "We have to keep moving."

Zayah hugged him tighter.

"Zayah," Arman wiped away her tears. "I ... I love you." He wiped away his own tears. "And we're going to find them. The real them."

She sniffed and glared into the distance, anger and determination painted on her face.

Uselessly lost, Arman let her lead the way. Zayah kicked, tore, and screamed profanities as she carved a path through the tightly packed Pilgrims. Arman and Zayah fought and clawed for every inch for what felt like miles.

Exhausted, bloody, bootless, and down to their bags and rags, Zayah and Arman stumbled out of the crowd onto the open road. They raced into the glittering vista, shepherded by the moon's glow reflecting off the stripes in the road. The illusions of Tara and Mona were nowhere to be found. He wondered if his real wife and daughter had made it through the pass.

Arman looked back at the eldritch god. Its hands rested peacefully in its lap, the third hand was raised in a sign of reassurance, and its eyes were closed.

Something ancient inside of Arman broke open. Something beautiful hidden beneath rainbows that spoke in the whispering language of butterflies. Something born in the wake of a terrible storm.

HOPE

Arman was certain Tara and Mona were alive and had made it over the mountain pass. He didn't know how, possibly a parting gift from the eldritch god.

He looked to Zayah and saw the same joyous madness in her almond eyes and Cheshire grin. They ran. They ran through the night until their feet were torn to ribbons, their bodies were numb from the cold mountain air, and their muscles swam in lactic acid.

Zayah collapsed with exhaustion. Arman cradled her in his arms and carried her like a baby. He walked until the sky spun from black into a nebulous haze of violet and indigo.

They bivouacked off the interstate beneath an outcropping in the cliff side as the stars closed their eyes to slumber.

Arman wrapped Zayah in a blanket. He held her with her head resting against his chest. The sound of her gentle breathing lulled him to sleep as he watched a silent sunrise.

Threads
by Kristin Marie Mitchener (Honorable Mention)

This story contains graphic descriptions of child abuse, domestic violence, and suicidal ideation that may be distressing or triggering for some readers. Reader discretion is advised.

From sitting alone in my bedroom playing with Cabbage Patch Kids so as to keep a safe distance from my mother, to ruminating about running away from the cursing and fighting, to wishing I was never born at all—Cabbage Patch Kids turned into alcohol, ruminations of escape transformed into a revolving door of volatile relationships, and wishing I was never born commenced into two suicide attempts, once at 24 and again at 27. It was while planning my third attempt at the age of 39 that I found my way back to my healing journey. It was also then that I had the painful realization that said healing journey had begun the very moment I, fresh and bloody from my mother's young, 20-year-old womb, took my first breath.

Alone and unwanted, hopeless and wishing to die. These are my earliest memories of when I was a little girl. My biological father was long gone after he and my mother divorced when I was one year old. He joined the army, moved to California and when he came back to Texas four years later, he was remarried. Throughout my childhood, he rarely called me, and I didn't see much of him despite us living in the same city. If it weren't for my great-grandparents making sure he stopped by to see me when I was spending the weekend with them, I'm not sure I would ever have seen him. And with my mother's extreme emotions and conditional love and attention, I was always confused about whether she ever truly wanted me around or even wanted me at all.

When I was two years old, my mother married Joel. I *hated* Joel. He wasn't my *real* dad, so naturally that made him my enemy. Eventually, my mother came to hate Joel, too. Their verbal vitriol progressed into push-ing and slapping, and I began witnessing physical altercations between the two by the time I had started kindergarten. During one particularly disturb-ing fight, my mother and Joel were wrestling on the living room floor in our house on Starling Lane. I was five and mere feet from the chaos ensuing before me. Biting at the neck of Joel's worn and faded t-shirt, teeth ex-posed, a small growl followed by saliva escaped my mother's lips. Instantly I was disgusted with her and ashamed that this living room floor was part of my home, that I was a part of *her*. Having watched their fights get more severe over time, I was terrified of what could possibly come after biting. I did what I was taught to do if I was ever in danger. On the push-button keypad of our corded telephone hanging in the kitchen, I dialed 9-1-1.

At some point while talking to a lady dispatcher, the fight moved into their bedroom. In what seemed like just a few minutes, a police car pulled up in front of our house. Through the living room window, I watched in fear for what was to come and remorse for what I'd just done as two police officers made their way up our driveway. I ran into my mother's and Jo-el's bedroom.

"Shit! Who called the cops?" my mother screamed as she peeked through the thin plastic blinds hanging from their bedroom's one small window.

"I did," I said, my voice and body quivering.

"God damn it!" my mother shouted at me, in a tone and at a level I had come to know as a signal for encroaching danger. Seeking safety and com-fort, I bolted to my room and got under my Strawberry Shortcake blanket. Soon after, I heard voices coming from the living room.

"Well, he didn't tell me Happy Mother's Day last week," I heard my mother say. After what seemed like only a few minutes later, a female po-lice officer slowly entered my bedroom. Surrounded by stuffed animals and hiding under a blanket, I must have looked exactly like what I was—a suffering, scared-as-hell little girl caught in the crossfire of two ill-equipped parents unable to maturely express their emotions.

The female officer had a gentle way about her. "Has this happened before?" Her voice was kind and caring, not like the voice I was used to hearing from my mother.

Peeking out from under my blanket, I lied, "No." I was scared that if I told the truth, I would be taken away. Surely *away* was worse than living here, so I chose to stick to what I knew best.

The police officers stayed a short while longer talking to my mother and Joel in the living room. After the officers left, as I lay in my bed with yet another traumatic wound inviting despair and loneliness to fester in my soul, my mother, her 5'6 frame hovering in the doorway of my room, said coldly, "Thanks a lot. Now I'm gonna have a record."

My mother wasn't arrested and Joel didn't press charges. She wasn't going to have a record, but I didn't know that as a five-year-old, and she *knew* I wouldn't know that. Her reason for telling me this was simple: shame me into silence.

Except for murmurs, the house was unusually quiet. Nighttime came. My stomach rumbled with hunger, but I was too scared to ask for something to eat. I went to sleep hoping the next day would be completely different—no screaming, no fighting, no more wishing I wasn't born—but completely different never came.

After seven years of fighting and two younger sisters later, my mother and Joel divorced, and we moved out of the house full of fighting. Moving into a new home meant a new school in a completely different school district. Even more jarring, I was entering public school for the first time after being in private Catholic school from pre-K to third grade.

It wasn't upsetting to leave my old school because I didn't really have any friends to leave. My exposure to mature situations at home resulted in my not being able to relate to other kids' imaginative, innocent affects.

It certainly didn't help that I was stick-thin thanks to my rabbit-paced metabolism, and I hadn't yet grown into my nose and feet. I was picked on by other kids because of my appearance and social awkwardness. Running up to me during recess, my Catholic-school classmates would yell, "Skinny Bones!" and "BigFoot!" I was a gangly outcast with inner chaos.

Children my age had scars from climbing trees and playing chase. Those weren't my scars. My pain was *so very* different. I had no father, no friends, and an emotionally absent mother holding my inner child hostage while slowly strangling me at the same time. *Empty, lonely, worthless, shameful* - this was my emotional state as a fourth grader and the state from which I would operate in life for nearly four decades.

The apartment had only two bedrooms. My two sisters shared the smaller room, which meant I had to share a room with my mother. She wouldn't let me decorate the room with posters, and she constantly went through my things, looking for more evidence that I was a rotten child. Within a few months of moving into the apartment, my mother's new boy-friend Chris began living with us. Chris was exceptionally tall and thin, had a ponytail and rode a motorcycle. He was a truck driver and a little rough around the edges. He was always kind to me and my sisters, and I felt he was nice to my mother. He called her "darling," often brought her cards and somehow, someway, put up with her emotional antics and outbursts.

For over two decades, my mother put Chris through hell. I often felt bad for the guy. She was so mean to him, hurling the most hateful words about his two sons, his manhood, and I was witness to it all. It was an extension of the environment while she was married to Joel. While their arguments never turned physical, the verbal aggression my mother displayed toward Chris when they argued was frightening. From what I came to know about Chris over the years, he had his own traumatic childhood from which he was operating out of—he wasn't raised by his biological mother, and he had no idea who his biological father was. Add that to my mother's traumatic childhood, which included not being raised by her biological mother along with having an absent father, and it's no wonder they had a tumultuous relationship.

Chris and my mother would go into what was supposed to be my bedroom, too, leaving my sisters and I alone in the living room to take care of ourselves. I'm flooded with memories of microwaving Bagel Bites to feed my sisters while catching an odd smell coming from under the bedroom door, the smell I would eventually come to know as "weed," emanating from the stench of her reprieve from being my mother. At night, Chris and my mother would sleep in the bed next to mine. As a pre-teen, having to share my sacred bedroom with my mother was cringe-worthy enough. Add to that the awkwardness of having to sleep next to a man to whom I had no relation. I had no sense of independence, privacy, or security.

My mother's fights with Joel continued, but fortunately they were only verbal. Lasting through their teenage years, she used my sisters as bait to get what she wanted from their father, which was attention and control. "We are following the visitation agreement word for word, and you better not be a minute late or I'm calling the police," she would yell at Joel over the phone. But when she wanted to party with Chris or go out of town with friends, it was different weather.

"Do y'all want to go to your dad's this weekend?" she would ask my sisters, in the most sickeningly sweet voice. Then she would call Joel up as nice as can be and extend the olive branch of *letting* him see his daughters extra for the week. And I was always lumped in with them when they went to his house. My mother never even asked if I wanted to go. I was confused why I had to go with my sisters to visit *their* dad, especially when she and I both hated him.

On the few occasions when I didn't go with my sisters, my mother dragged me around with her, whether or not it was an appropriate setting for a child. Mostly we'd go to Chris's friends' houses where he and his guy friends would drink and smoke cigarettes and marijuana.

If we did do something specifically for me, the day almost always ended with my mother hacking, "After all the time/money/effort I spend to make you happy!" Happiness felt selfish and was too hard to come by anyways, so I learned to stop trying.

One day we were driving in my mother's beat-up, old, maroon Fairmont, which had a busted air conditioner. It was a typical Texas summer, and my legs were sticking to the vinyl seats. We were on the way to somewhere Chris was at, because weren't we always? I noticed she had started smoking cigarettes. As a fourth grader in the nineties, I was in the thick of D.A.R.E. at school and learning to "Just Say No!" to drugs, alcohol, and cigarettes. To my curiosity and concern, I asked her why she smoked cigarettes.

Windows down with cigarette in hand and the ends of her long brown hair whipping in the wind, my mother replied, "'Cause all of Chris's friends smoke."

Lightheartedly repeating what she had told me in the past, "If everyone jumped off a bridge, would you?" I asked.

"Shut up!" she screamed, in *that* tone and at *that* level. Another mother message delivered swiftly: never challenge nor question her behavior. Once again, she shamed me into silence.

While I didn't see it at the time, and definitely didn't feel it at the time, being forced to go to my sisters' dad was one of the few positives in my life, the others being my strong relationship with my great-grandparents and my budding relationship with the Lord.

Time with Joel provided relief from my mother's extreme emotions and what I now know to be neglect and abuse. Time away from my mother's behavior also gave me time to process her behavior. I saw how she treated Chris, I saw how she manipulated Joel, and I experienced her verbal and emotional abuse constantly.

Over the years, I began wondering if my mother was the abuser, or at least the primary instigator of violence, when she and Joel were married. This was a radical shift and one that was difficult to contend with as I had always, since my earliest memories, viewed my mother as a victim. If she wasn't the victim, then maybe Joel wasn't such an enemy after all.

Joel came from a close-knit, loving family. From the time they met me as a two-year-old, his family always included me in events and did what they could to help me feel part of the family. After Joel and my mother divorced, his family continued to accept me and show me love. Visitation with Joel regularly included visits to his parent's house, Grandma's and Grandpa's, where everyone, which included Joel, his five siblings—all sisters, married, with countless children running amuck—would gather to cook tamales, play board games like Trivial Pursuit and Taboo, and just spend time together whether it was Christmas or a Wednesday. I would watch the interactions between the Morenos, especially between the spouses. They used their inside voices, and there wasn't any arguing, only laughter and storytelling.

During one of our many visits to Grandma's and Grandpa's, one of Joel's sisters pulled out his old journal from middle school. "I did the jig with Martha!" he had scribbled in pencil in the somehow-still-assembled, wide-ruled notebook from what seemed to me at the time to be the Stone Age. We all passed around his journal, laughing hysterically as we each took turns reading a different line. I caught a glance of his eyes, and they were glassy with tears.

I can still feel the ache of my heart further softening for him at that moment. Threads of love and acceptance and togetherness were being woven together to create the fabric of hope, which would continue to drape me as I traveled along my healing journey. The Morenos were proof that my path could take a different shape than my mother's patterns of abuse and instability I was accustomed to surviving.

Fast forward to November 13, 2015: my wedding day. All five of Joel's sisters were there along with their spouses and countless cousins from the Moreno clan. I was walked down the aisle by Joel, who by that time I considered to be my dad.

My mother's words told me I was rotten, less than, inherently defective. She would get in my face, so close I could smell her breath, and yell, "You have no idea how I was raised. You have it *good*." She always accentuated the *good*. Her mantra was, "I want you to have a better life than I had."

Then she used this desire for a better life for me to tell me how much she's done for me, is doing for me, and how much I don't appreciate any of it. I wasn't a good sister/daughter/student/friend. "Smile more. Wipe that smile off your face. Stop being such a worrywart. You need to take things more seriously. Go play with your little sisters. Act your age." More mother messages internalized: I needed to be different from and better than who I was.

My mother depended on me to meet her ever-changing needs. I was expected to make her happy, feel appreciated, and better her day and her mood and her life. That's a lot of pressure for a five-year-old...a fifteen-year-old...a twenty-five-year-old. Love and acceptance were awarded to me when my behavior was deserving of such, and it had nothing to do with things within my control like making good grades or keeping my room clean. When my behavior resurrected her wrath, she rejected me with different tactics.

As I grew older and my priorities and needs changed, her tactics changed accordingly to make my punishment and rejection even more degrading. The most minor of offenses warranted her cursing and screaming the meanest things. "I can't wait for the day you turn 18! I'm going to *travel*!" She still had two younger daughters; why did freedom have to come to her after *I* was gone? But her silence, this was always the most deafening defeat.

My mother perfected the art of depriving one sister of attention and affection while doting on the other two sisters in front of the identified "bad" child. It was a merry-go-round I did not want to get on, and I was on guard all the time because I knew my turn was coming up, and my turn came up more often than for either of my sisters.

"I can't stand to even *look* at you!" she would yell before banishing me to my bedroom. I would wait for her permission to eat, anxiously waiting for the knock on my bedroom door signaling I was worthy of food. Sometimes the knock never came. I would go to sleep, afraid of what might happen if I went into the kitchen to make something to eat.

Sometimes she would put all the food away and yell from the living room, "Come eat dinner if you want it." How embarrassed and ashamed I felt pulling out the Tupperware containers, reheating the food and eating by myself at the kitchen table with my head down while she sat in the living room watching television with my sisters and carrying on as if everything was fine, as if she wasn't slowly killing me inside. This continued until I moved out of the house at 18.

My mother's rejection created a fierce yearning for love and acceptance from the friends I did make in school, and I needed them to communicate this love and acceptance repeatedly. This is a tall order even for the best of friends. Using my internal sensor developed as a child, I would sniff out friends' "true" feelings about me, which I always feared and assumed was more rejection. I would hurt them before they could ever hurt me, to the point where they no longer wanted me in their lives. I searched endlessly for the feeling of being wanted. And in all the wrong places. Namely, with boys. When one boy would show me attention and tell me nice things about myself, I would fall head over heels and think he was the person I would spend my life with. I felt wanted and loved and gave away the most sacred part of myself. Time and time again, I never learned my lesson. Finally, *fucking finally*, after never being enough for my own mother, was just too enticing to pass up. I allowed myself to be used and used until I was no longer useful. Abandoned and worthless is how I entered and exited every friendship and every romantic relationship.

After hearing my mother for 18 years tell me she couldn't wait until the day I turned 18, I graduated high school and got the hell away from her. I knew college was my way out, so on to college I went. My mother's abuse continued from afar. She would call my dorm room, pick a curse-riddled fight with me, and then hang up on me. This would be followed by days, sometimes weeks of her ignoring me. She also liked to make threats. "You think you're so smart? I'm not filling out your financial aid paperwork, so good luck going to college!" she once screamed before hanging up on me.

During the middle of my freshman year, I finally had enough of her hanging up on me. One evening as she proceeded once again to demean me with her sailor's mouth, I hung up on her. She called me over and over again for hours, and I wouldn't answer. The next morning, as I walked into my 8 a.m. English class, my professor scurried toward me.

"You need to call your mother," my professor said.

I was stunned, literally speechless. Why is my professor telling me to call my mother?

She repeated herself. As I opened my mouth to say … anything, she added, "I don't want to know."

My mother had called the university security office that morning and said she hadn't heard from her daughter and that I wasn't answering my phone. Campus security contacted my professor to let her know one of her students was possibly missing and to confirm if I was in class that morning. Humiliated, I called my mother after class. I listened in disbelief as she recounted how afraid she was in telling the dispatcher that she couldn't reach me.

"I didn't know where you were! You answer when I call you," she demanded, without any acknowledgement of her behavior.

With each passing semester, a little more distance would grow between my mother and me. I was outgrowing her antics, her punishments, her idle threats. I was outgrowing *her.* However, my mental health challenges persisted. I hadn't yet realized that I had suffered trauma during fundamental stages throughout my childhood. I was running and hiding and operating in survival mode every day. I failed classes, abused drugs and alcohol, and made poor choices about who I let into my life. It was during the fall semester of my junior year of college when the harder substance use—which had progressed in less than six months from one night per week into nearly every night of the week—took its toll on my mind.

I had recently seen a university psychiatrist because my depression was more severe than ever before in my life, and I began contemplating suicide. Going to the university psychiatrist was the worst decision I could have made. What seemed like getting help turned into being treated by a doctor who chose to give me ample supplies of benzos and antipsychotics, at no cost, even after I expressed to him I was having suicidal thoughts. A few days after my second appointment and complimentary refill of medications, I attempted suicide for the first time.

While my boyfriend at the time was in class, I got into my bed and wrapped myself up in the handmade quilt gifted to me by my great-grand-mother, just like I had my Strawberry Shortcake blanket as a child. All the medications my generous psychiatrist had prescribed me were in white paper bags on the floor next to my bed. I grabbed the bags and began opening bottle after bottle, pouring pills by the handful into my mouth.

Within what seemed like mere minutes, my heartbeat sped up to the point where it was pounding, contracting painfully like I had never felt before. Gagging, I continued forcing pills into my mouth until I couldn't swallow any more. Soon I felt like I was going to vomit. *I don't want someone to find me in throw up*. After five or so minutes, I couldn't hold back my vomit any longer. I felt the urge to go into the bathroom, so I hurried to get out of bed. Instantly, my legs gave out, and I fell to the floor. Crawling to the bathroom, I could only feel my arms pulling me forward, my elbows digging into the carpet and my torso dragging across the floor. Once in the bathroom, I slid myself to the toilet, leaned over the rim and began puking up pills. I felt them traveling from my stomach up into my throat and out of my mouth. I kept looking up at the bathroom's frosted window to see the "white light" signaling the end was near. The white light never appeared, and the side effects were just too much to endure. I gave up trying to give up. I called 9-1-1.

I don't remember what I said but soon after calling, I heard an ambulance outside my house. I had managed to make my way into the living room and onto the couch. Two male paramedics entered the front door.

"She's tachy," one of the paramedics said, after placing a stethoscope against my chest.

They asked me questions about my medication and doctor. I was in the midst of poisoning myself and somehow convinced the paramedics that I was merely experiencing severe side effects from new medication I hadn't taken before. They felt my boyfriend could take me to the hospital, and they recommended I call my doctor. As the paramedics left, I remained slumped on the couch.

"Do you think you need to go to the hospital, or do you want to call your doctor?" my boyfriend asked. He, too, believed the story I told the paramedics.

Calling my doctor would not have been an unreasonable thing to do in that situation. But I knew the truth. "I need to go to the hospital."

Still unable to walk, my boyfriend carried me outside and placed me in the front passenger seat of his red Chevy truck. On the way to the hospital, he didn't say anything. He just cried.

By the time we reached the ER, I had started losing consciousness.

The next memory I have is being in a room where I heard typical hospital noises like beeping and a lot of voices talking. A female voice said they were going to place a breathing tube down my throat.

"No, I don't want that," I slurred.

"You're going to have to keep your eyes open then," the voice said.

"Okay," I replied, with full intention of trying. And I did as best as I could. I had heard stories about having to drink charcoal or having your stomach pumped. I didn't have to suffer through either of those. I was given an antidote through my IV and wheeled on a hospital bed to a small room. A nurse sat beside me for hours.

I was so tired and just wanted to sleep, but anytime my heavy eyes started to close, I heard the nurse say, "Keep your eyes open."

When I was finally discharged that night, the doctor said I overdosed.

"But you weren't trying to hurt yourself on purpose, were you?" he asked. He looked at me.

I knew what to say. "No," I answered.

"Suicide is not a label you want to put on yourself. And you were almost successful."

When I got home, I stayed in bed for days. I was ashamed to show my face to my boyfriend or friends. I told them I had a reaction to the medicine I was taking. That was my story. I can't imagine anyone believed it. It was too late in the semester to withdraw from my classes, so I received "F's" in the five classes I was registered for. I never saw that university psychiatrist again. I stopped taking the medication and spent the rest of the semester abusing drugs and alcohol to escape the pain of being me.

Still, I persevered in pursuing my college degree. Spring semester following my suicide attempt I re-enrolled in the five classes I had failed. I took full course loads during both summer sessions and completed five more classes in the fall. My depression persisted, but so did I. My grades were a mix of B's, C's and D's, but I was managing to knock out class after class even amidst the binge drinking and substance use. I was determined to finish.

Finally, I reached my last semester of college. My boyfriend and I had started going to First Baptist Church near campus. While I was raised in the Catholic church, during my teenage years I attended a Baptist church in my hometown and really enjoyed it. My boyfriend was raised Baptist, so it was a good fit for us both.

At every Sunday morning service we attended, I wept. The leader of the college ministry was Pastor Bruce. His sermons told me I was whole and loved, just the way I am. He told me the Lord can restore the most broken-hearted. At the end of each service, Pastor Bruce would invite anyone in the congregation who wanted to make Christ their Lord and Savior to come up to the altar. One Sunday, after a full service of weeping, I heard Pastor Bruce extend his weekly invitation.

Snot ran down my nose, and I tasted the saltiness of the endless tears flowing down my cheeks. "I think I need to go up there," I told my boyfriend.

"Do you know what that means?" he asked.

We both knew what it meant. The drugs, the drinking, the terrible arguments had all run its course, and it was time for a change. I realized I could no longer go on the way I was—depressed and suicidal. I wanted something more. And I knew "more" was possible only through the Lord.

As I walked down the sanctuary's main aisle, my weeping continued, but a smile had formed on my face. I reached Pastor Bruce, and he leaned toward me. As the music played in the background, he whispered to me, "What is your name?"

"Kristin," I managed to reply. "Kristin, tell me what brings you forward today." Everything came out—I told him about my suicide attempt, my depression, my fractured childhood. He prayed over me and ushered two females to take me to the side of the altar where I would talk to him more after the service. We scheduled a time for me to come to his office that week to talk about my decision to dedicate my life to Christ. On February 10, 2008, as I stood in waist-deep water holding my nose so as to not inhale the holy liquid surrounding me, I looked at Pastor Bruce. He nodded to me.

It was time.

I closed my eyes and was immersed in unconditional love and forgiveness. As I emerged from the water a new creature, threads of faith, truth, and surrender wrapped themselves around my soul once knotted with sorrow. My fabric of hope was the strongest it had ever been in my life. *Things will be different now.*

Two days away from my college graduation, an affair seven years in the making, my mother was pulling one of her usual telephone stunts to gain sympathy, attention, and control.

I'd had enough. "You're my mother, and I love you, but I don't want to talk to you for a very long time," I said with firm confidence before hanging up. I have not spoken to my mother since this day 17 years ago.

Complete disengagement from my mother was not an easy decision to make, and it has not been an easy decision to keep but it was the right decision I stand by to this day. Mother's Day and my mother's birthday are both difficult days to get through each year. But anytime I feel the yearning to reach out to her, I remind myself of her toxicity and total unwillingness to take accountability for her actions. I have wanted to scream so many times to her, "I am the *child*!" No matter my age, I will always be the child, and my mother will always be the adult. She will always hold the ultimate responsibility for her behavior and how she treated me.

Upon graduating from Texas Tech, I began working as an editor and writer for a small corporation. My boyfriend and I broke up after two tumultuous years together. I moved out of the house we were sharing and into my own apartment. I knew I needed to heal from my mother if I was ever going to have a healthy relationship.

I began seeing a therapist who recommended I read the book, *Understanding the Borderline Mother,* by Christine Ann Lawson. It was like reading the story of my life: the beliefs I had about myself, the way my mother treated me growing up, her words and actions and distance and smothering, my moods, her moods, how I lived each day of my life, how I treated people, how I managed my relationships. My eyes opened to the fact that I was not the awful, unworthy person my mother described me to be. I had received emotional justice. This book was also a mirror, and I realized I had been perpetuating what I desperately needed to escape.

I decided I was going to take my love for reading and combine it with my quest to heal. I read several more books about borderline personality disorder and emotionally absent mothers and healing from childhood trauma and neglect, such as *Will I Ever Be Good Enough?,* by Karyl McBride, *Healing Your Emotional Self*, by Beverly Engel, and *The Emotionally Absent Mother* by Jasmin Lee Cori.

I was introduced to terms and ideas such as inner child, adult child and inner critic. Before reading these books, I never considered myself abused or neglected. My mother never physically hit me, and I had clothes to wear, food to eat and a bed to sleep in every night. How bad could my life really have been? Physically I survived, but she wounded me mentally and emotionally with her words and rejecting behaviors. *That* is abuse.

She failed to give me the love and compassion I needed to grow into a healthy adolescent and undermined any development of self-confidence and self-acceptance that are critical to becoming a fully functioning adult. *That* is neglect.

Once I realized this was my truth, that my inner worth has nothing to do with my mother, I felt such relief, such redemption. Intertwined threads of knowledge and insight were further spun into my fabric of hope. For about a year, I continued therapy, attended a Baptist church that I really liked, and trained for a marathon. My depression still reared its ugly head with random irregularity, but the suicidal thoughts had faded. *I was healing.*

One night as I was nearing my apartment door after walking my dog Rowdy, my neighbor from the upstairs apartment in the building next to mine came walking down the sidewalk. I hadn't met this neighbor yet, so I waited for him to come nearer so I could introduce myself. "Hi, I'm Kristin, and this is Rowdy."

"I'm Preston," my neighbor replied.

Small talk ensued. "So where did you go to school?" I asked him.

"Texas Tech."

I was surprised in the most pleasant of ways. Since meeting my ex-boy-friend, I had always envisioned us going to college football games together, cheering on our alma mater we shared, the alma mater where we met and fell in love. That dream ended when our relationship ended.

Something very special will come of this, I thought.

We said goodbye, and Preston continued down the sidewalk toward the parking lot. I went inside with a big smile on my face. Threads of friendship, connection, and possibility were being stitched into the fabric of hope that was enveloping me to my core.

Preston and I began hanging out shortly after our meeting. I wasn't interested in getting serious with anyone. I told him this, and he felt the same. So, we just spent time together as platonic friends. I opened up to him about some of my struggles with mental health but never revealed my suicide attempt. I was too ashamed and afraid he would no longer want to be my friend.

He was a great listener, and wise beyond his years. We would joke that he was my life coach. And in many ways, he was. He was my comedian, my shoulder to cry on, my sounding board. Over the months, our time together increased, and I began to develop romantic feelings for Preston.

After going out one night, he and I made our way back to his apartment. Overflowing with liquid courage, I told him I liked him. He said he liked me, too. Something very special was happening indeed.

The second time I tried to end my life, I was 27 years old.

After a night of binge drinking, I repeated my first attempt. I emptied every pill bottle of my prescribed medications. I hastily scribbled on a note-pad, "It was never enough," placed the note under my pillow, and passed out likely not long after.

When I woke up the next morning, I forgot what I had done. Until I tried getting out of bed. Planting my feet on the floor, I attempted to stand, and an electric shock ran through my body. I collapsed like a rag doll on the floor. I stood back up and another shock zapped through my body, and I again collapsed on the floor. I clawed my way back into bed and passed out.

At some point, my friend randomly stopped by my apartment to check on me. She was with me the night prior and saw how upset I was, not to mention drunk.

"Kristin! Kristin!" my friend shouted at me.

I opened my eyes and saw her standing in my bedroom doorway. There was no way for her to get into my apartment unless I had left the front door unlocked last night. I was confused and disoriented and must have looked as such.

Familiar with my mental health struggles, she began repeating, "Did you take something? Did you take something? Answer me!"

I couldn't form words. I couldn't piece together a thought. Then I lost consciousness. Flash forward to the next memory I have, and we are on the bathroom floor. She held me in her arms as I had seizure after seizure and went in and out of consciousness. *I was dying before her very eyes.*

My friend did what she thought was best. She carried me back into my bedroom and placed me in bed to let me sleep it off. I could have gone into a coma or simply never woken up again.

At that time, Preston and I were no longer dating, but we were still hanging out and talking regularly. My friend called Preston and told him what was happening. He rushed to my apartment, and he stayed there until I gained consciousness. He didn't say much, just sat in the living room until the side effects of my poisoning my body had subsided.

I never went to the hospital or sought medical treatment, even though I had what felt like shuddering in my brain for a month following my suicide attempt. I just continued living as if I hadn't tried to kill myself again.

Twelve years after my second attempt, I started planning my suicide for the third time. I was on the cusp of turning 40 years old and had recently resigned from a job I loved because my depression had taken over my life.

Preston and I had been married for six years. He saw firsthand the toll depression took on me over the years. He never judged me or shamed me or left me, the latter of which I would have understood and something I honestly expected. Just like he had just over a decade ago, he waited in the background for me to get better. He also became my caretaker, feeding me homecooked meals, getting me into the shower and taking care of every single household chore while I spent weeks at a time in bed. I am so thankful we did not have children to witness my despair and utter helplessness.

Day after day, I obsessed about suicide for hours, holed up in my bedroom searching Google for pictures of people who had hung or shot themselves. Shame and isolation fed my depression, and depression fed my shame and isolation. This cycle of pain was endless, and my sadness was consuming me. The only way to end my pain was to end my life.

I knew pills were an awful way to go, as evidenced by my prior two attempts, so I decided on hanging myself. I researched where the pressure of the knot should be on my neck to bring about quick unconsciousness. I read how the body thrashes about as it leaves this world, and you must be sure you aren't interrupted before the act is completed because you could be left with permanent brain damage. Being a vegetable sounded like a worse case of pain than what I was experiencing. *This had to work this time.*

I started practicing hanging myself. Looping a scarf around my throat and attaching myself to the doorknob, I would slowly transfer the weight of my body away from my legs and onto my neck.

During one practice session, my efforts started to work. I became light-headed and for several minutes saw black spots every time I opened and closed my eyes. It was during this practice session that I truly understood my death was becoming a reality that would soon come to fruition. I decided *the* day would be my birthday. My rationale was that I wanted my birth date and death date to be the same. Leaving the world exactly 40 years to the day I was thrown into this shitshow gave me a sense of control, bringing me more peace about my decision.

I detailed the plans of my death in my journal. The thought of everything coming together to create my death felt beautiful, peaceful. Suspended, floating away to somewhere that wasn't *here*.

I created a death playlist with the songs I wanted to hear playing until unconsciousness took over. I knew which door I would use, the left French door of my home office.

My final letter, the all-illusive "suicide note," was written and ready to be folded into a small white envelope I found in my husband's file cabinet. In my note, I gave instructions on what to do with my body and my belongings—cremate me, sell everything to help with final expenses and donate the rest. I specified where I wanted my memorial service to be held. My note was a combination of apologizing to my family and telling them not to make this about themselves.

They have no idea, I thought, taken aback that they didn't suspect I was ending my life soon. They are going to be shocked. But they shouldn't be. *Did they really think I was going to make it?* There just didn't seem to be enough I could say or the right way to say my final words before leaving forever. I ended the letter with, "Maybe some people just aren't meant to be here."

I cried and yelled at the Lord, who I had begun doubting even existed, "Why have You let me get so far gone *yet again*? You know every hair on my head, and You are letting me go through this shit as part of Your "master plan." I began resenting God.

It was during one day's death doomscrolling that two random websites popped up: one site was a rather amateurish-looking suicide prevention website; the other was an article about ketamine IV infusions for suicidal ideation.

On the suicide prevention website, I read about near-death experiences from survivors of suicide attempts. They all said that they felt like they needed to go back to Earth, to finish *something*, although they didn't know exactly what it was. There was also a letter written to a female victim of suicide by the victim's best friend. "Do you know how hard your mother cried for you that day?" she asked her dead friend.

While my mother and I had been estranged for 14 years at that point, that sentence stuck with me. I visualized my mother at my funeral. Her obese frame was cloaked in black, face bare of makeup and pale in disbelief. She couldn't stop crying. I couldn't stop her from crying because I was dead.

I then started seeing other people at my funeral and found myself wondering how they would feel about my death. I was empathizing with my loved ones. My husband would be a widower at 35 years old. I left the funeral I had created in my mind feeling a bit of unease regarding my decision to end my life. It wasn't that I was completely having second thoughts about killing myself, but I was having thoughts *other than* killing myself.

Reading the ketamine article was the pivotal turning point of my life. This article explained that the off-label use of ketamine had been shown to be successful with treatment-resistant depression. I also read that it was fast-acting, providing relief from acute suicidal ideation within just one or two IV infusions. I re-read my suicide note, and there was so much anger and confusion behind it, anger and confusion I would be leaving my loved ones to process.

I started thinking how sad God would be if I gave up on myself. Giving up on myself would be giving up on Him. I just picture Him looking at me and asking, "Did you not think I would protect you? Did you not believe I had good things planned for your life?"

I made the decision to ask my psychiatrist, who I had been seeing regularly for two years and who diagnosed me with bipolar depression, about ketamine treatment at my next appointment, which was one week away. I was about one month out from my fortieth birthday.

"I've heard great things about ketamine. Is this something you want to try?" my psychiatrist asked.

All the threads that had intertwined themselves throughout my life—love, acceptance, forgiveness, faith, truth—wrapped like a cobra around my soul. With my whole heart I answered, "Yes."

My psychiatrist wrote down the names and phone numbers of three ketamine clinics. As soon as I got home after my appointment, I sat down at the kitchen table, cell phone in hand, and started dialing. I called the first two clinics. No answer by either, so I left voicemails.

I had one clinic left to call. In classic physician handwriting, I read the words, "Spring Center of Hope." I dialed the phone number and within a couple of rings, a woman's voice answered. Like the lady police officer who came into my bedroom when I was a frightened little girl, the woman, who I would come to know as Wendy, was warm and caring. After receiving the pertinent details regarding the ketamine infusion process, I made an appointment to begin my first treatment the very next week.

My ketamine treatment plan was twice weekly infusions for six weeks. Within two treatments, the urge to practice hanging myself and intense hopelessness began to subside. I had completed three ketamine treatments by the time my fortieth birthday arrived. While I remembered this was the date I had chosen for my death, I didn't have the desire to act on it. My birthday came and went, but one thing remained—me.

Over the weeks, I also had what I considered "bad" treatments, where my depression felt intensified during or immediately after the treatment. However, within two to three days, I would be feeling better. After six weeks, I received infusions with slightly less frequency—once per week for several weeks, followed by one treatment every two weeks, and further spaced apart according to how I was responding to treatment and how I was feeling.

As time progressed, so did my mental state. I did have sporadic set-backs when the suicidal thoughts would return. During those times, I would call the ketamine clinic and say, "I'm feeling suicidal."

Without judgement, Wendy's kindness extended through the phone. I never had to wait longer than one week from the day I called to receive an infusion. The ketamine never failed to pull me out of the darkness. Spring Center of Hope saved my life.

Now I sit contentedly in my office, the same office I was going to hang myself in, three years after rehearsing my death. When I think about how far I have come since the years surrounding my bouts of acute suicidal ideation, I often find myself asking, "*Why me? God, why did you let me live while so many others have been successful in their attempts?*

While only the Lord knows the full and exact answer, I believe I am meant to be here. I am meant to be alive and I have a purpose to carry out. Sharing my story to help others who are hurting, I believe, is my purpose.

I continue to receive ketamine infusions every three to four months because I have continued to struggle with suicidal thoughts. I've realized that there's no "one and done" to treating my mental health. It's a continuous act of faith and godly persistence. The difference today is that I allow my pain to empower me and not overpower me.

Fabulous fabric of hope, indestructible by the grace of God, pulls me deeper into my healing. It provides strength and comfort as I let go of my woundedness and the specialness it provides me, and I find my identity and uniqueness in who God created me to be.

My journey as a wife and mother can now really take shape, and take the shape *I* want for my life and my family I am building—swirling patterns made with bright threads of nurturing, unconditional love and wonderment, all intricately woven together to create hope.

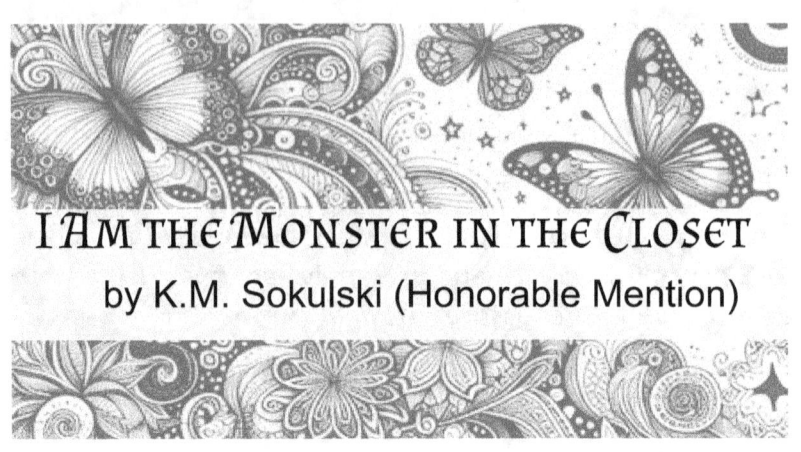

I Am the Monster in the Closet
by K.M. Sokulski (Honorable Mention)

This story contains graphic descriptions of self-harm that may be distressing or triggering for some readers. Reader discretion is advised.

I'm becoming the monster in the closet.

It's two thirty in the morning. My husband's asleep in the bedroom. I hear him snoring faintly through the walls of the closet, and the master bathroom between.

Today marks the sixth night I've been pulled from my bed with a terrible quivering in my arms, anxiety-induced palpitations and vivid re-imaginings of my fifteen-year-old self caught in an obvious lie. It was twenty-two years ago, and I can't remember what the lie was. My brain's catalogued feelings and regrets rather than accuracy and meaning. It doesn't matter.

It's two thirty in the morning according to the watch I purposefully—but *shouldn't* have—left on my side table. My therapist discouraged me from keeping time-telling devices at my bedside. I kept my watch by my bed to squint at when this happened, anyway.

Once more, I've given in to the newly established nightly routine of rising from my bed shaking with the anticipation of what my activated amygdala's already set in motion. It's later than that now. So, I've already started a new day.

My husband didn't hear me when I emerged from our bed, smoothing the sheets and placing the decorative pillows with a finality that I wouldn't be returning to sleep. He never hears me when I retreat around the foot of the bed, unlock the bathroom door with my thumbnail and embark on the silent journey into the little square closet at the end of our L shaped bathroom. The ritual is complete when I reach the monster's den. I push back the perpetually open closet door so I can sit down on the floor and lean against it.

Then comes the transformation.

New mother of a beautiful boy and wife to a gentle soul with a heart for philosophy and hands rough from labor and toil by day. By night, a savage monster lurking within a closet. I remind myself that I have the full-time mom experience. I have it all.

Perfect baby.

Perfect husband.

Perfect life.

Maybe this time I can rein in the monster. Maybe this time I can blot out the monster's fanfare, as my therapist suggested. The transformation is slow at first, after all. A moment frozen by anticipation that offers brief seconds for my frontal lobe to make its final case before the rest of my brain spirals into its savage assault.

The monster's torn us into separate entities, my brain and I. My brain's assumed the role of the gentle conduit of logic, forgiveness and a hint of self-empathy.

Too bad it's attached to me, a maelstrom of emotional disarray and reawakened trauma with an expertise of repressing *it* instead of the monster. Sleep deprivation makes it harder. My unrelenting ADHD relegates the effectiveness of my frontal lobe to that of a deacon trying to give a sermon in a fishbowl. Anxiety attacks are my daytime inconvenience. As in the 'normal waking hours' people who don't have this problem would refer to. This isn't in that window.

Adrenaline ravages the blood in my veins, my stomach sinks, and my face prickles as my body initiates the monster's transformation. I won't be blotting out any fanfare this time. It isn't a physical change but a chemical one. The mind is always slower to it. The logical part of my brain is holding out as if somehow the rest of its conjoined self will realize the error of its ways and show me mercy. It'll run through the sentiments all three of us agree on, despite the state we're in.

Locking the bathroom door at night was a great way to cut off access to the temptation of retreating to the same place. My hopes that I couldn't manage jimmying the lock with my fingernail were dashed when I unlocked it on the first try. There's no keeping me from the monster's color-coded den of fine-enough hand-me-downs, shoe racks lined neatly with equally fine-enough shoes and purses straining from being hung for too long from hooks. The monster claimed its den and I always want out. I always want to hurry up to the part where these rituals become distant memories.

Postpartum depression, my therapist called it. You have a mild case of it. I call it the monster. A monster that is *anything* but mild. It's more common in women diagnosed with ADHD. My fate was sealed the day I innocently filled out a questionnaire at my newborn's six-month wellness checkup and his pediatrician came to the room with gentle words and plenty of encouragement. Fast-forward seven months, and I still haven't reined in the monstrosity that's taken to gorging on me.

My fists clench and unclench. The stems of my fingers vibrate from the ritualistic instruction of forming a fist. Self-harming used to be a distant stranger to me. Something symptomatic of a hormonal teenager convinced she was unloved and living on borrowed time. Something I'd already worked through.

My arms won't move yet. I still have enough presence of mind to plead with my brain to not give in to the monster. To show me mercy. My frontal lobe mutes with a last attempt at echoing my therapist's words. The behavior is unnecessary.

The monster isn't necessary.

My fist flies hard at my thigh. Hard and precise. Enough to entice the blooming pain of a freshly forming bruise from the spot where my knuckles struck. A wordless negotiation. Just the one and I can go back to bed. It can count as a step forward. A very small and pathetic step forward. We can forgive a slip-up. A fluke that stops at just a fluke.

Satisfaction isn't achieved. Since I've already managed the strike, attempted negotiation results in a green light for the monster's favorite pastime.

My heart's in my ears. I'm vibrating. Pain blossoms randomly across my legs, my arms. Adrenaline powers the force behind my strikes. My brain provides the maelstrom that fuels the monster's need for physical release.

I am the monster in the closet.

Self-harm is a learned behavior. No child grows up with this behavior. Someone did this to you, and the dependency on brutality comes from trauma. My therapist described this to me with a gentle word and an air of compassion I wish I currently shared for myself. A questionnaire filled out with thoughtless honesty at my child's pediatrician first exposed the monster's undetected intrusion. My therapist simply gave it a name.

The monster stops suddenly, interrupted by the frontal lobe's attempt to communicate by way of Morse code through each throb of my eardrums. It, of course, only manages a brief distraction with the faintest reminder that this compulsion isn't necessary. It's not too late to stop.

The monster's quick to deafen and even quicker to locate another striking point. The monster has its own voice. A bombastic resurrection of compulsive behaviors I thought I'd left behind. We're in the monster's domain, after all. It's a pitch-dark box mostly soundproofed by walls stuffed end to end with fine-enough clothes that smother the percussion of its ritual.

Your baby deserves a better mother, the monster tells me. *Barely made it six months and you're going crazy. Medication doesn't work on fuck ups. You're not grateful enough for what you have. If you were, you wouldn't be doing this. Only freaks do this.*

A handful of the monster's favorite scriptures it prefers to spew in my mind. Some nights, it gets tired and begrudgingly allows me to return to bed—the sentence served. Most of which results in fitful sleep littered with freshly catalogued regret. This is not one of these nights.

Sometimes, the monster is careless. Loud. Loud enough to make the door jostle enough to squeak. Wrestling for control, the monster and I listen to the still quiet. Each of us expecting a different outcome. The sound of the door either rouses my husband, and the inevitable groan of the mattress announces his emerging, or the pregnable silence remains.

Triumph leans in my favor when the quiet scrapes of my husband's bare feet on the bathroom tile tell me he's on the way. I'm huddled against the door with my aching arms wrapped around my legs, heart pounding and face buried from the shame of what the monster compelled me to do.

Of what *I've* done.

Of the fact that this ritual involves a third party now.

He envelopes me in his arms, offers me gentle words.

But I'm still under the monster's spell.

The scent of eucalyptus wafts off his neck, the whisper of his aftershave lingering on his cheek. The difference between our body temperatures is ridiculous and I all but shiver in the heat he radiates on me like a burning sun in pitch darkness. The senses ground you in your present moment, as my therapist says.

It's all bullshit, my husband says. Your mind is feeding you bullshit. You're a great mom. An amazing wife. You don't deserve what just happened.

I want to believe it's true. I want to believe so badly that one day I'll *know* it's true. The monster thinks differently through the twitch in my fingers as my fingernails dig deeper into my arms. My husband stops it with a firm wrench of my hands from my arms. He's been a part of this ritual long enough that I've tethered a particular form of shame to him. It's not supposed to be like this. It's not supposed to feel like this. My too-perfect baby, who sleeps through the night shouldn't be doing so in a house with a mother like this.

I don't want to be the monster in the closet.

It takes doing; mild negotiation, the persuasion of his gentle words and my husband pulls me up by the arms, spreads his arms around me and guides me back to the bedroom.

The monster's resentful. Hates being interrupted, and the intrusive thoughts threaten another maelstrom in my head. The only one I'm willing to utter is the one where I tell my lifelong partner that he should have me committed. To which he always responds with the same, simple answer.

No.

It's sickening that I'm as dissatisfied as the monster, still deeply under its spell. His simple answer is challenged. My baby can't grow up with a mom like this. What happens when he can see that his mom does this? That his mom belongs in a madhouse?

To which he replies, this is all just bullshit your brain's feeding you. You're the one under assault right now. Your brain is attacking you. You aren't in control. *None* of this is your fault.

A bout of stubbornness and shame keeps me anchored to the floor, but before long, my husband's pulling me by my arms and we return to bed together. He holds me until he falls asleep, and I stare at the wall, too exhausted to slip from his arms but awake enough that I know I'll be here for a while.

I don't want to be the monster in the closet anymore.

I force myself to echo my husband's gentle words like I'm preparing to recite a limerick. A faint whisper amidst the monster's relentless chorus in my head, but the practice eventually pays off. I manage an hour of sleep.

By six in the morning, I'm pressing on my contact lenses because I have to start my day. I try again to echo in my brain what my husband said to me hours before. It's not my fault. I'm not in control.

I pissed away my time, answers the monster as soon as my echoing starts. *We had all that time to sleep, and we didn't use it.*

I'm used to insomnia, so a deep breath, an extra cup of coffee at breakfast and I start my day. All the while, the monster repeats its words about wasting the time I had to sleep in the back of my mind like a battle cry.

Then the monster tires and I sober.

My little one's up by the time I'm throwing away my paper plate, bare of the sad little store-bought bagel with cream cheese it once cradled. I enter my son's realm of green, lushly painted trees on the walls and little foxes gathered in the form of murals and stuffed animals, all matching the charming forest theme.

He greets me with an impossibly infectious smile, cobalt blue eyes sparkling at me as if my emerging from behind the door is an unfathomable miracle I'm not appreciating enough. He bounces on legs concealed by a sleep sack of pastel green and soft cotton that makes him look like a beanie baby.

It's going to be a good day, I tell myself while simultaneously greeting the eagerly bouncing thirteen-month-old who boldly releases their uncertain hold on the deeply chewed railing of the crib. I catch him beneath his arms in time and off we go. It's fine that I wasted my time to sleep. Baby's in a good mood. I can feel it in the way his muscles contract as he kicks happily to transition from his bed to my arms. Especially since Dad fed him breakfast and put him down before making for the garage. In the brief quiet, the monster attempts several mild strikes. *How tired is he? How badly does he want to go back to bed? You should have let him—*

Little fingernails swipe at my chin as I carefully lay my son on the changing table. He finds my face fascinating this morning as I peel the layers of his sleep sack and later cotton, dinosaur-patterned pants to change his diaper. All the while he smiles between babbles, offering me an unintelligible conversation I'm happy to respond to with some noises of my own. I can handle today. It's only night three of no sleep. I'm out of the monster's haunting hours, I can worry about that losing battle later. I just have to be functional for my son during the day.

He smiles so easily later when we make it to his playpen. I stack a tower of his little toys, and they come tumbling down. I lay my head on his chubby little lap, and he beams down at me with an exaggerated smile that always reaches his eyes. He doesn't understand if it's a game I'm playing or just a cuddle, but he's mesmerized and eager to find out. God rewards mothers with boys so they can learn the meaning of unconditional love.

I've been reminded of that countless times from the moment I discovered what he would be. Learn the meaning of unconditional love. It's not fair for him to have to teach me, especially when the monster has no intention of surrendering its game.

He pushes off and crawls across the living room carpet towards his wooden barn with little cut-out holes of farm animal characters and begins to try to pluck the goat from a human-sized hole. He babbles, tilts his head in confusion and keeps trying. I watch him, hear him moan in frustration, begin to get up from where I'm lying down on the rug, and the tantrum starts.

He throws himself back in a fit of uncontrolled rage. My hand barely shoots out in time to catch the back of his head before it can connect with the rug underneath him, and he sobs, face reddening. Three kicks to the barn and the toy tilts over, spilling its contents every which way, coveted wooden goat included. He's shrieking with the beginnings of what I'm grasping at the meaning behind the phrase, "toddler rage" and I tell myself to stay calm. To ignore the quickening of my pulse, the vibration of my exposed eardrums. My breath catches.

I forgot my earplugs in the other room.

The little lilac-covered siphons my therapist recommended to take the edge off of my child's agitating screams aren't in arm's reach. It's too late. I'm triggered. I haven't been triggered like this since my PTSD's reprieve in my early college years where history partially repeated itself with a bottle of scotch whizzing past my head, a punch to the nose and the day my ex-boyfriend decided to prove himself a man.

My son's cries aren't the same thing. They're unrelated. Innocent. He's not my ex-boyfriend. Somehow, he hits the same, agitating pitch—a shattering bottle or a thin-lipped mouth shouting at me inches from my nose, and it all comes back.

The surface of my face prickles as what's passing through my ears rattles my brain and I lurch forward. I dig my nails into the carpet on either side of my toddler, who squints up at me with eyes stained pink and cheeks glimmering with translucent streaks. He's wailing up at me, and I'm paralyzed. The monster's desperate to take action. The bruises hidden beneath my jeans radiate with remembered pain. My nails ache with the force in which they're being pressed into the hard weave of the carpet. If I wait long enough, I can vividly picture them tearing from their stems.

I'm not breathing.

The monster spews at me while I wrestle to control arms that have gone numb, kneecaps that bloom with the pain of digging themselves into the vinyl floors just beyond the edge of the carpet. *You're a horrible mother. You're letting him cry helplessly underneath you while you just sit here. He deserves better. You don't love him enough. A better mother wouldn't have forgotten the damn earplugs.*

My better judgement's fogged by the mental assault ravaging my head. My frontal lobe attempts to distantly drone its counterargument in my head, between the spaces of the monster's spewing. It's not true. This isn't a moral failing. You're not in control.

My son rolls over onto his left and clutches at my right arm, little fists clinging to me for the comfort I should already be giving him. My brain's dwindling attempts to uplift me from the monster's constant bombardment proves about as effective as the teacher in the *Peanuts* cartoon.

I'm failing my child.

Agreeing with the monster always comes with a bitter taste on my tongue and heat boiling in my veins. My little one kicks repeatedly at my thighs, and I remember what my psychology-obsessed husband told me happens to a child when they've cried for too long without any form of comfort.

They lose hope.

The painfully familiar thought offers its own form of panic that releases me from my paralyzed state. The monster all but mutes inside me. My body remembers how to move while my mind is still reeling, remembering how to quickly gather my flailing child in my arms. I bring him to my breast.

It's ok, I tell him. Don't give up hope. Don't give up on *me*.

He curls his little body around me, arms latching about my upper arms, legs straddling my torso. His head falls on my shoulder, and I'm rocking us back and forth. Don't give up on me, I beg.

The monster's enthusiasm for the opportunity to remind me I'm a liar manifests in a new form of disgust welling inside of me. I'm asking my son not to give up on me when I gave up on myself a long time ago.

My husband comes in from the garage, his arrival as timely as it is uncanny. He asks me if I'm okay, and I only then realize I'm crying. Pathetic, the monster sneers inside of me. *It's his day off and you're making his day miserable. Can't you even handle your own toddler?*

Let me take him, my husband says, hands already wrapping around my son's little torso. I don't want to. I want to make it right. I want to correct the mistake I've made, but my mouth clenches shut. My son wails again in disagreement at being peeled from my chest. His cries vibrate my eardrums, and I can't take it anymore.

I shoot up from the floor, seized by the unwelcome compulsion to retreat. My husband calls after me. I shoot back that I don't want my son to see me like this.

To see his mom like this.

I ignore my husband's attempts to reassure me and my baby's shrieking after me. It's not lost on me that he's watching his own mother turn his back on him. I'm shattering his tiny world before his very eyes. What a horrible mother and wife I am. The monster celebrates as I make for the bedroom, increasingly hating myself with every step.

The monster takes me back to the closet.

I hate that I'm here. Hate that I keep making it back here. Hate that I've regressed back to the very ritual I'm trying to kick. I was happy during pregnancy. In awe of the little life growing inside me. The perfect baby. The fighter. The high-risk hurdles he overcame every step of the way. The living proof I was capable of doing something right. Of doing something *purely* good.

They're out there, beyond the thin walls of the square-shaped, color-coordinated closet of mine. I'm boxed in. Contained. I can hear the faint sound of my son laughing. My husband chuckles, followed by the clatter of plastic tumbling. My stomach sinks inside me with the resentment both me and the monster share. They're living out there. Delightful giggles, precious moments, seconds spent bonding with one another—and *I'm* sitting here missing all of it. My fist clenches, but I resist the itch spreading across my muscles to let it fly. These are the waking hours. I'm not supposed to be like this right now. I medicated this morning; I'm not supposed to be giving into this so easily.

When do I stop being the monster in the closet?

The monster revels in the question as if in challenge. *You deserve to miss it. They're better off without you there. Stay out of the way and let them bond. Those memories are for people who actually love themselves. You don't deserve—*

The door from the bedroom clicks, and we both hitch. The monster quiets, as if it were possible for it to get caught. My head lifts sharply from my folded legs because I at once wonder if my son's been left alone. The footsteps can only belong to my husband. The monster ignites a spark of irritation in me, an accusation ready on my tongue about leaving our child alone in the other room. My forehead throbs from how hard I was pressing it against my kneecap. Then they enter the monster's den.

Now we're *all* in the monster's closet.

My husband greets me as if this is the most normal situation in the world. My son beams at me, Gerber Baby smile in place, as if every ounce of anxiety and trauma tethering me to this place is complete nonsense. The monster hates interruptions. It lashes out before I can hold my tongue, telling him to get out. Telling them *both* to get out. I remind him I don't want my son to see me like this. He deserves better. I don't deserve to have a son suffer this.

My husband smiles, his eyes crinkling with more than a degree of sadness or pity and he turns to our son, stating they have to cheer poor Mom up. My son laughs, waving his arms with a burst of energy as my husband lowers them both down to join me in this pathetic little den.

No sooner does my husband sit down on the ground than does my son reach his chubby little hands towards me with expectation. His smile stretches impossibly. *He doesn't understand*, the monster says, but a small part of me feels like he doesn't care.

The same part of me delves deeper. He heard everything during pregnancy. He heard me pray repeatedly for him alone in the bathtub to take his gamble on me. There's nothing I wouldn't give. It hurts to remember the promises I made. Vows to break the patterns, the cycles of abuse I inherited with anything but grace. The very same I'm struggling to keep now.

My son chose the monster in the closet, and the monster wants to be chosen again and again.

The brush of tiny fingers against my forearm is all it takes for me to unfold my legs and take my son into my arms. He gives me a breathy, satisfactory chuckle as I wrap my arms around him. My body has a mind of its own while the monster continues to compel my brain into its gluttonous desire for punishment. His little palms brush the bruises on my arms, and I'm not sure where the betrayal I feel within me falls.

My body for never rejecting my son when he reaches for me? No, that's the miracle. The monster for stealing precious moments by sequestering me to sate its vicious amusement? More likely.

I don't want him to see me like this, I remind my husband. My body holds him tighter, and my son rests his chubby little cheek on my breast. He stares up at me, smile wavering with the comprehension something is happening, but never flinches. Our eyes connect, and he smiles again with a wisdom I'm projecting onto him that he isn't afraid. That he's aware of my anger and pain. I allow myself the thought that it makes sense. After all, we *were* connected once. He knows all my dirty laundry.

His little hands brush more bruises on my arms, and I bite at the corner of my mouth to keep my lip from quivering. He turns his head, exploring the faint tapestry of purplish-green smudges that came before the sweeps of his little fingers. He knows. He sees. He sees what the monster's done in this closet.

My husband smiles at all of this, something that makes me want to disappear from the guilt that gnaws at me. This time I've managed to drag the *entire* family into its den. The monster's desire to get me to spiral into another bout of self-loathing is interrupted by my husband tickling at my son's foot, earning a surprised giggle. In a cutesy voice he tells our son, poor *Mahm* is having such a tough time, she needed her little *bebís* to cheer her up.

My son coos as if in agreement and gives up on exploring my dotted arms, standing up on his chubby legs to hug me with his whole body. Something he learned some time ago from all the repeated, wiggling hugs I gave him until he was breathless from laughing. I think to the future, in the moment of soft clarity. The times I want to have with him. Picturing when he begins to talk, what we'll say to each other when he can speak. Inexplicably, an equally uncomfortable truth comes with my husband and baby's presence in this tiny little closet.

I don't have to be the monster in the closet.

A reminder of what should have been obvious but unfathomable mere moments before. I did all this for nothing. None of it was necessary. The monster isn't necessary, and I've come back to the beginning again. Only now the monster has intruders. One in particular I was once tethered to.

The tether's still there, though. Much to the monster's disappointment. I won't do that to him. I hate it enough that I do it to either of them.

My husband stands, taking my son back as he does, telling me it's time to come back with them. I don't resist, and my son peeks at me from over his father's shoulder, only to retreat to pop out and start a game of peeka-boo. I play along, unbridled joy sounding in each overly animated giggle my son lets loose from beyond his father's shoulder.

I let out a breath, exhausted but mildly entertaining the thought of leaving the monster behind in the threshold of the closet. Picture it in the form of a cheesy, non-threatening *Goosebumps* creature with its cartoon-ish arms crossed across its chest, stewing in its abandonment.

The image helps a little, and I allow myself to listen to my husband's reassurances. Your mind's feeding you bullshit. You're only just starting your medication. You're a great mom. You're my wife and I love you. A tiny, near-microscopic semblance of hope sparks inside of me. A thought man-ifests in my mind that I'm slow to entertain, but by the time the bedroom door closes behind me I'm repeating a new mantra.

One day I'll stop being the monster in the closet.

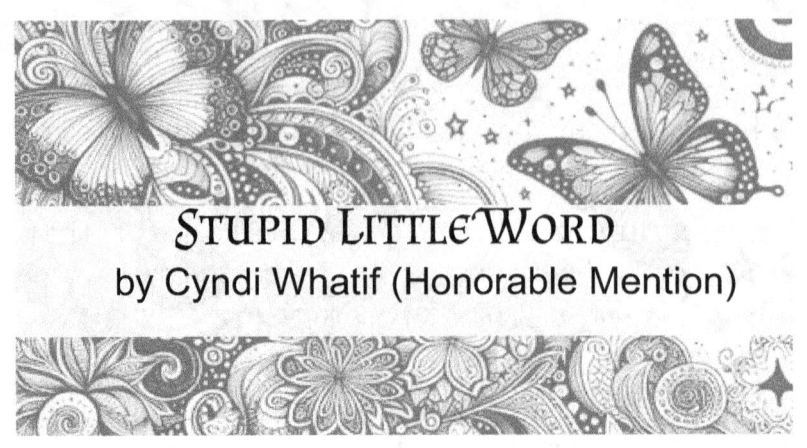

STUPID LITTLE WORD
by Cyndi Whatif (Honorable Mention)

Hope. *What a stupid little word*, I think as I open my eyes.

I was slowly becoming aware of the fact that I had fallen asleep on the couch ... again. I lay there for a moment, fully aware of my dog having sandwiched herself between me and the couch back. If I move, she moves, and the day will have to begin. Opting to just not start my day, I linger for a few moments, but my bladder reminds me of why I woke up in the first place.

So, I begin my morning routine: take the dog potty, start the coffee, sit down in front of my computer and open my email. My eyes quickly scan for any potential replies from the ten jobs I had applied for yesterday.

I mentally note the need to unsubscribe from at least a dozen newsletters. But I never do. Why? Because of that stupid word: hope.

When you know something must change before something can change—but you don't know where to look to find that change—you end up looking everywhere.

I scroll down until I see yesterday's dates showing up.

Nothing. *Again*.

Sigh.

The coffeepot beeps to inform me the brewing is complete. As I return to the kitchen, I can smell the roasted beans before I can see the full pot, my tiny black shadow in tight pursuit. She follows me everywhere I go ... all the time. I'm her new person. Kihap was our daughter's little dog, left behind when she moved out. *Was it truly over ten years ago?* That must mean Kihap is getting up there in her years—halfway through the double-digits now, I guess. Almost blind. Only half her teeth are left. But she still loves to eat.

She knows the morning routine. I don't feed her until I go to get my second cup of coffee, which is why she's following me slowly into the kitchen instead of racing ahead. In fact, her plump little body doesn't even follow me across the threshold onto the cracked tile floor. She comes just close enough to the kitchen to keep me in her limited sight. I wonder if I'm mostly just a silhouette to her now.

I quietly pour my coffee and take it to the couch to read. After I settle into my worn spot on the couch, she makes multiple attempts with her short legs to join me. She finally succeeds. Today she noses around the blanket draped over my legs, searching for an opening. She finds one, and I feel her cold nose touch my thigh as she burrows in.

I read. I pray. I plan my day. I scroll through job feeds. I think, *How can there be 44,300 remote jobs available and I can't get chosen for a single one?*

I try not to count how many I've applied for. I try not to think about how far into the interview process I've made it—three times now.

Nothing.

This morning, I feel like Kihap looks: tired, worn down, and not really making an effort to go anywhere or do anything. I give her a soft pat under the covers. *Am I all washed up too?*

I torment myself with each application I fill out, picturing what it would look like to have one of those jobs. I wonder what it would feel like to have enough money to make it through the month. The whole idea builds to the point of a smile sneaking onto my face as I think about the possibilities—the hope. The hope that was now flickering out inside of me from trying for so long. *Is my candle reaching its end? How many more times do I want to be ghosted?* Rejected. Passed over. Or some other less-harsh wording of the reality of not being chosen.

Of the endless cycle not ending.

Of change not coming.

I let out a sigh. Based on the reaction of Kihap's head popping up, though still covered with my yellow blanket, tells me it's part of my routine. Evidently, I must audibly exhale before I get up to get my next cup of coffee. Her little head bobbing and nose sniffing, trying to find the entry point she created a little while ago. I fling the blanket off my legs and set Kihap free. She morphs into a little puppy, all full of glory and energy, as she catapults herself over the ottoman and begins dancing on her two hind feet as she attempts to tell me where the kitchen is, as if I didn't know. *Is she even the same dog? How could her countenance change so much so quickly?*

My standing up causes her body to explode with even more excitement. She begins whining and sneezing and contorting her body as she makes jump after jump. *Are her feet even touching the ground in between those jumps?* She runs into the kitchen only to run straight back out again to see if I am following her.

When I do, she starts running in circles from one end of the tiny kitchen to the other. When I bend down to pick up her bowl, she starts circling laps around my feet, making it difficult to walk. I place her bowl on the counter to fill it with food. She uses this as a cue to start barking at me. It's like she needs to tell me how to do it. This particular morning, it annoys me because I don't want her to wake anyone in the house.

I find myself talking to her. "Can't you see I'm doing it? Why are you barking at me? You don't need to tell me what to do. I'm doing it whether you can see it or not."

As soon as I say it, I pause and then close my eyes and laugh. *Is this how God feels after my protestations and concerns I poured out to Him not more than ten minutes ago?* I shake my head and tell myself, *lesson learned.*

If something needs to change, then something needs to change. Maybe a remote job isn't what would be best for me even though I think it is. If I believe God answers prayers, maybe he is holding the remote door shut on purpose. Is that why the door's stuck shut? I'm reminded of the backdoor to the house that always requires a good bit of tugging before Kihap can go outside. Well shit, I have been pulling on this work-from-home door for a year and a half now! *Is God saying wrong door and I am just ignoring Him?*

Absent-mindedly, I place her bowl of food on the ground and think about my revelation. Before I'm able to pour my second cup of coffee, she is done—happy and searching with big sniffs to see if any fell out of her bowl and onto the floor during her frenzy of eating.

The funny thing about the stupid little word hope is the way it comes in and out of our lives. Hope isn't always a sudden slamming of a door. Oftentimes, it's just a gradual fading into nothing. We cling to it and don't realize it is still slipping away from us. We only realize it was missing once it is found again.

I set my coffee mug down on my desk and begin my job search again. This time I won't include "work-from-home."

The sun goes down, signifying the end of another day. Unfortunately, the forever-hopeful, food-loving Kihap doesn't know the evening routine for meals. Probably because there really isn't one. Sometimes I feed her after I eat supper, while other times, if I am going somewhere, I feed her before I leave. But there is a problem with this. I think she is getting doggie dementia, if that is a thing. Anytime I move from my spot during the remainder of the evening, she acts like she does when I am about to feed her—even if I already have.

"Don't get your hopes up, Kihap; you already ate," I say.

She doesn't understand and refuses to believe it when I tell her she *has* already had her supper. Over and over again. Sometimes three times in one evening. It's not because she is hungry; she just doesn't remember being fed and she loves to eat. Kihap thinks if I'm up, *"It's time to eat. Yippee!"*

I envy her. Forever hopeful, whether the hope is substantiated or not. I watch her on her roller coaster ride of anticipating supper and then not receiving it—though technically she has, but she just doesn't remember it.

Dejection crashes onto her face as she watches me sit down again without filling her bowl. How she hangs her head as she follows me back to the couch where she stands with her chin down, eyes up, and the short, reluctant wagging of her tail almost between her legs. Apologizing. Wanting me to lift her up onto the couch next to me though I know she can jump up. *Did her hope fleeing deplete her so much that the jump she could make in the morning was impossible to fathom now?*

Is hope really that powerful?

I think about all the jobs I have applied for today, refusing to imagine landing one of them or what it would be like. Not wanting to feel the pain of lost hope again like I currently see in Kihap's whole body. That type of hope hurts...or should I say cuts? She is bringing it on herself, but she can't help hoping. *Do I just go through the motions and look at it like it is a numbers game?* That would be the same as having no hope, wouldn't it? Hollow.

Out of habit, I numbly check the emails on my phone. One sticks out. A request for an interview for the next day! The energy that rushes into my soul and surges to my brain catches me off guard. I try pushing it back down to my stomach, but it won't be denied. Hope has shown up again. It is begging to breathe. I don't have the heart to suffocate it, and yet I don't know if I have the strength to let it grow either. Thus, I am hurled back into no-man's-land, where having little to no hope is better than having no hope at all.

I guess hope is that powerful.

The Gift of the Trees
by Ricki Wegner (3rd Place)

After the war

They tried to erase us

From public spaces

They dragged us from the streets

Took our right to learn, to gather, to speak

Said our voices were dangerous

And should not be heard

So we whispered to the wind

The wind carried our words

To the trees

And the trees

They remembered

Layla's body ached as she strained under the weight of a large bucket of water. This was her seventh trip to and from the river, something she did every morning under the scorching desert sun. She should have been in school, but had aged out two years ago, the day she turned thirteen.

This was according to the laws of the land. Laws that she did not grow up with but were enforced by the new regime that came into power several years before. Laws that did not apply to her older brothers, who continued with their studies and were taking their education completely for granted.

She sighed bitterly. If only her father were here. He would understand. He had been a scholar and a poet but fought bravely to protect his people. In the end, he was killed and their family devastated. He would have understood how she stewed inside anytime her brothers complained about coursework when she longed to be in their place. She had inherited his passion for learning new things. Oh, how she loved school. She daydreamed about it as she walked from the river to her family's mud-baked house on the edge of a mountain. She imagined being back in her simple but cozy classroom, sitting on the front row, raising her hand, scribbling furiously at her desk, breathing in the smell of books, paper, and ink....

Layla was quickly jolted back into reality by the sight of a Watcher stationed at his guard post. She avoided eye contact, looked down at the ground, and tried to make herself small. She hated having to do this, but she'd had her ankles beaten with a stick for drawing too much attention to herself when she was younger. And now that she was getting older, she had to be more careful, or she might be left with more than just bruises on her ankles. She held her breath and walked on. Slowly, but not too slowly. Stiffly, unnaturally. *Be invisible, be invisible, be invisible.* Beads of sweat broke out on her face, and not from the sun.

This chore fell to her because, out of everyone in the family, she was uniquely suited for this task. The age of a girl determined her freedom. By Layla's next birthday, she would only be allowed out of the house if accompanied by a male guardian. Since her brothers were in school, and she was the youngest of the sisters, this task fell to her and her alone. She did not mind, though. Layla loved the small taste of freedom that she got from splashing her feet in the cold stream. She loved the sight of the desert dunes shifting with the wind, and the birds soaring high above. And she knew this kind of independence would be gone soon. She felt it slipping away with each passing day.

She almost stumbled. She could feel the Watcher's eyes on her as she passed by, and she held her breath yet again. Everyone feared the Watchers. They had been sent by the new rulers post-war. The claim was that they brought stability to what was once a land in chaos. But instead, they brought fear, oppression, and governed with an iron fist. No one could step out of line. And it was the women who suffered most of all under their reign.

The Watcher let her pass by. Layla didn't realize how tense her whole body was until she turned the corner and exhaled loudly, feeling her shoulders relax. She set the bucket down and leaned against the wall of an old, bombed-out building, noticing that her hands were shaking. She gave herself a moment to rest, looked up at the sky that shimmered from the heat, and wished to be one of those birds overhead so she could fly far, far away.

But though the routine was the same, today, after all, was not like any other. It was her birthday. Memories of happy celebrations from her childhood swept through her mind's eye, and she ached for yet another thing that had been taken from her people when the war was lost. The new regime forbade such celebrations and banned music and dancing.

She was still daydreaming when she arrived back home, set the bucket of water in the courtyard, and sat down, letting the sun kiss her face. She loved the family courtyard. It was wide and spacious. Trees, plants, and flowers were scattered throughout, the greenery bringing life and peace to a harsh environment. The walls were tall, which meant the Watchers couldn't see in, and she was free to be herself.

"We've been waiting for you, Daughter!" Her mother emerged from the doorway. Layla's grandmother trailed close behind. Normally, at this point, her sisters would come spilling out of the doorway, eager to hear tidbits of news from outside the home, but she heard her grandmother shooing them back into the house.

"We haven't forgotten, you know," her mother said, embracing her.

"Forgotten what?" Layla feigned, playing along. Of course, they hadn't forgotten her birthday. Celebrations may not be allowed, but their family always found a way to honor one another's special day.

"That fifteen years ago on this day, you were born," her grandmother declared. "We have seen you grow from a girl to a young woman, and we are so proud of you."

"Layla." Her mother's tone shifted to something more serious. "We sent everyone away because today we have something to share with you. There is a secret we have been waiting to tell you, and today is the day you are now of age."

Layla was intrigued.

They took her hand and guided her to the area of the courtyard that was scattered with trees.

There was the largest one, the one that she'd grown up climbing. The oldest one, whose branches had drooped with the weight of suffering that had blanketed the land during the war. The steady one that grew an abundance of pomegranates, no matter whether the rain was good or not that year. The one that was so beautiful that every kind of bird would come and rest on its branches and sing to the sky. And the small, unassuming one that she had never paid much attention to. This was the one they directed her to.

They sat down, and her mother started a small fire while her grandmother made tea. The fire danced and sparked, an invitation to sit, talk, and listen. Layla had always been captivated by fire. For generations, her people had told stories by firelight. It was their way to pass down their traditions and history and honor the memory of those who'd gone before them. No matter that it was already hot. The fire set the mood and ensured they had an abundance of tea.

They were silent until the tea was ready, as if pondering carefully the words they were going to say. At last, it was ready, and her grandmother handed her a steaming cup. Her mother spoke first, with a voice that was soothing and gentle, as is true for all mothers.

"After the war, they tried to–"

"She knows this part already!" Her grandmother interrupted.

"But she loves this part. The children know it by heart, her most of all."

"She's not a child anymore," Layla's grandmother said.

"You're right." Her mother turned to Layla, who smiled at their bickering. Though societal rules demanded the silence of women, it was never that way in their home. Everyone in the household spoke their mind, which meant constant disagreements. But it also felt exactly how things were supposed to be.

Her mother began again. "You were younger then, but you saw how they banned us from work and school and took away our hope of a future. Our crime for such punishment? Being born a girl. We wept. We wept so fiercely that the heavens heard."

Her grandmother, a practiced storyteller with a melodic tone, spoke next. "One night, as a mother cried over her daughter's stolen future, a star fell from the sky and landed in the dust at her feet. Her tears watered it and up sprang a magical tree. As this tree sprouted seeds, the birds came and scattered the seeds all throughout the land.

"These trees were unlike any other. They remembered. They listened. They communicated. When a woman placed her hand on the tree, she was instantly given the ability to understand and speak in the language of the trees, which is not bound by distance, but tethers souls together no matter where they are. And so, the women became connected to the memories, stories, songs, and sorrows of one another. They were no longer isolated. And the most dangerous thing to those who tried to rule over us was born."

"What is that?" Layla breathed, even though she knew what they would say.

"Hope."

"Layla, this is more than a tale that we whisper to you at bedtime. The magic is real. And today we would like to share this gift with you. Can we show you?"

All her life, Layla wished magic were real. When she was younger and read children's books, she would close her eyes and try her hardest to transport herself into the story she was reading. Tales of adventure, magic, and battles of good and evil. As a young girl, when her father told bedtime stories with monsters, dragons, and spirits, she could see with vivid imagination the kingdoms he built with his words and wanted more than anything in the world to experience magic in this life.

And here she was, being told that it was real and a gift for her to use.

Not once did she question whether this was possible. She just knew.

"Yes, show me," she breathed as she reached out and let them place her hand gently on the rough, earth-colored bark of this tree that she had always overlooked. She heard a low hum and felt an awakening of ancient energy. Then, in her mind, a flash. Brilliant light, more vivid than any dream.

Are you ready to hear the songs of your sisters? A whisper, not audible, but imprinted on her mind. She closed her eyes. *I am ready.*

A tidal wave of images crashed into her.

She saw hundreds of women and beautiful, glowing threads, forming a web that connected them to each other.

She saw a woman who'd been beaten, rising from the ground with fire in her eyes.

A newborn's wail. The midwife whispers, *It's a girl.* The mother, exhausted, kisses the baby's forehead. *I will protect you.*

A woman in prison, barely able to touch the tree outside the window of her cell with the tip of her finger. *I do not regret resisting, but it is dark and lonely here. I just need someone to tell me I am not alone.*

You are not alone. A voice called out to the woman in prison. *We are with you. Your sisters are with you.*

Layla gasped. *Can I speak to them? Will they hear me?*

Yes, the tree whispered.

The power of this magic was breathtaking. It was as if one beheld the beauty of a night sky but had the ability to zoom in on any star they chose. She found the thread that connected her to the woman who'd been beaten, gently pulled on the thread, and called out to her. *Can you get to a clinic?*

I cannot leave my home, the woman replied.

I'm so sorry you are in pain. Can I help? I once read in a book how to make a healing salve from common ingredients found in the kitchen. Turmeric, garlic, honey, fresh olive oil .... She listed off the ingredients and shared how to prepare and apply the paste. Getting to use knowledge she'd learned to make a difference for someone made her feel alive again.

I am grateful. Thank you, my sister. There are others like me who need to know this. I will tell them.

Layla pulled her hand away, her heart pounding, and sat in stunned silence as the images faded from her vision.

They were connected. Every woman who had ever touched this kind of magic tree, scattered across the dusty streets, hills, mountains, rivers, and roads. They could communicate.

Up until now, Layla had not cried. Not while she watched her mother forced to return home, the doors of her dream job slammed in her mother's face. She did not cry when the Watchers beat her ankles for them accidentally showing in public when a cool breeze swept up her long dress. And she did not cry when she was told that girls her age would no longer be allowed to go to school and to receive an education, even though she had been crushed. For all mothers, out of a fierce, protective love, taught their daughters to guard their emotions so that the eyes of the Watchers would never turn towards them.

She had held it in so well. Until now. Now the tears came violently. Her shoulders shook with grief that had been suppressed for so long. She half expected a rebuke from her mother or grandmother for such a strong display of emotion. But instead, they embraced her.

"From the moment our freedoms were taken from us, we vowed we would resist. You deserve a future. We deserve a future. The heavens answered, and though we have not been able to return to our rightful place in society, we press on, and we will not be stopped."

"My sisters?" She asked.

"They know."

"My brothers?"

"They do not know yet. This secret is dangerous. We are very careful about who we share with, and when. We are not sure who among them would stand with us and who would turn against us for having such powerful magic. The Watchers have been attempting to poison the minds of men against us."

Her heart withered just a little. How could everyone not see how wrong this was? For a human being to be seen as less than another? How could some of her own brothers not be trusted?

"Take heart, dear one," her grandmother said. "Kingdoms rise and fall. It is the way of this beautiful and bitter world. There will come a time when those ruling over us will come crashing down. But for now, this gift is yours and is something they will never be able to touch."

They held her and sat with her as her tears flowed like rivers. Soon after, her older sisters came trickling into the courtyard where they sat shoulder to shoulder. Understanding was in their eyes. They did not sing songs to celebrate like when she was a child. But they wove flowers into her hair and shared cakes sweetened with dates and honey. And as she smiled because the cakes were as delicious as they'd always been, her tongue tasted a new flavor mingled in. The salt of her tears.

Her purpose was renewed. The tree gave Layla hope for the first time in a long time. Every day she would sit by the tree, bring her hand to it, and connect with women all over the land. She discovered that everyone had something to share, and so the women were able to keep learning in secret. They no longer had access to books, but the knowledge they shared with one another became a living library. They shared knowledge, stories, poems, joys, sorrows, and warnings.

One day, a woman needed help. She was in the pains of childbirth, with no healing house nearby and only the other women in the family there with her—none of them trained in childbirth complications. *Something is wrong,* one of them spoke through the tree. *We need a midwife. Can anyone find us a midwife?* The network lit up with communication. A midwife spoke. *I am too far from you, but I know exactly what to do, and I will talk you through it.*

Layla witnessed in amazement as, despite all odds, the baby was born safely. The collective was there, honoring this moment with their presence, their togetherness. A healthy baby. A baby boy. The mother kissed him. The collective spoke a blessing over the mother and her innocent, pure child. For him, the blessing was everything the Watchers said a boy should not be.

May you be kind and humble

Brave and selfless

May you always reach for others

When you feel lost and helpless

May your heart be tender towards those who are scared

And for the times you have fear

Know that we will be here

For the times you feel pain

Know that you can shed tears

May you know you are loved for all of your days

And may you lift up those around you

Along the way

Tears filled Layla's eyes as she thought of how the gift of the trees had saved the mother and baby's lives. And though her people still faced great difficulty, this moment gave her hope for their future.

Many more moments like this came to pass. But alas, their troubles were far from over. The Watchers sensed the shift. Though there was no outward resistance, it was clear that they were losing the control they thought they had once wielded.

And so they dispatched spies. They pressured and coerced men to turn on their wives, sisters, mothers, and daughters. And while there were many good men who stood with the women and wished for their freedom, there were others who began to view women through the eyes of the occupying government. Deserving of invisibility and silence. Inferior.

Though they could not understand exactly how the women could channel the language of the trees to communicate with each other, they heard rumors of magic and were determined to root it out.

In the end, all it took was one man. One man, who desired to receive honor, accolades, and wealth from the Watchers, took aside his young son and commanded him to ask his sister to show him the magic. This boy, not understanding the consequences, went to his sister. He was amazed when she showed him that if she placed her hands on the tree, she could communicate with women all over the land.

"Try it with me," she said, hoping that he, too, could experience this gift. She placed his hands on the tree, and hers over his, and they both closed their eyes. Only she saw the images and heard the whispers.

"Tell me what you see," he said, disappointed that he couldn't experience the magic.

But how does one describe a sunset to someone who has never seen color? She shared with him as best as she could. And when they took their hands off the tree, she told him that he must keep it a secret, or it could be dangerous for many people.

He went back to his father, intending to keep it a secret, but his father grabbed him by the shirt collar, pushed him against the wall, and yelled at him that he needed to stop acting like a coward and speak up. The boy was terrified and told him everything. When he had finished, the father let him go, and he lay crumpled on the ground, sobbing, as the father strode away in the direction of the Watchers.

The betrayal brought swift action. The Watchers were sent out to cut down all the magic trees. Women tried to warn one another through the network, but nothing could be done to save the trees. Those who were able to, gathered seeds and hid them. The people were stunned. For a second time, the dreams of women were snatched away. In every city, women and girls were ordered to go to the public square and were forced to watch as the Watchers lit a fire and burned up every last tree.

The smell of smoke filled the land, and that day, something both terrible and wonderful happened. The loss of the trees and the communication was devastating. But then the women looked to the right and left of them, and saw that many men had decided, against the Watcher's wishes, to stand with them.

"We are with you," they said.

They, too, had preserved seeds from the trees. They, too, wanted a land where opportunity and freedom belonged to everyone.

And so time passed. The trees were replanted in secret and began to grow again. Mothers whispered the tale of the trees' magic to their daughters and also their sons.

"You are not meant to be hidden," they told their daughters.

"You must never forget," they told their young sons. "Your sisters are like you in so many ways. They are full of ideas, dreams, and a compulsion to do the things that they were made to do. To use their minds and their voices and not hide them away. Stand with them, my sons. The world will be all that it is meant to be when boys and girls can stand shoulder to shoulder as equals."

And the boys listened. And though they could not understand the language of the trees, they could understand love and hope. Hope of a future so bright for all of humankind, that even the stars themselves would be amazed.

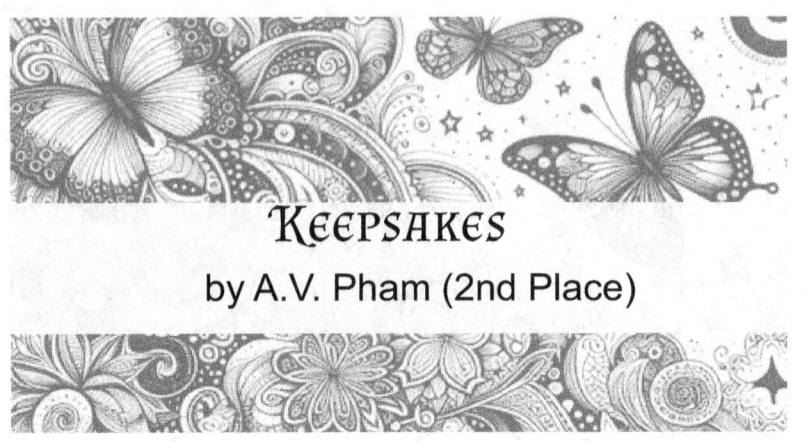

KEEPSAKES

by A.V. Pham (2nd Place)

It started with a chain. A thin gold strand with a small pearl landing daintily at the crook of her clavicle. It caught my eye before I followed it upwards to the slender neck, pointed face, and nest of wild, flowing curls at the top of her head. Amber's gaunt cheekbones and hollow eyes did nothing to conceal how beautiful she was. Hauntingly, devastatingly beautiful. Or maybe I'm just drawn to broken things.

That's been my whole life, constantly feeling the need to fix things and make them whole again, sometimes better than the original. Puzzles, Lego blocks, dollhouse furniture, always with the building and gluing and connecting. It's why I picked the career I did. I'm a death investigator for the district attorney's office. Before that, I was a crime scene investigator. Crime scenes were like puzzles to me and the victims and their families, broken pieces I could put back together. At least that's what I thought I was doing. But when you've been in the business as long as I have, you realize not all crimes can be solved, and not all broken things can be fixed.

I met Amber Banning on the eve of my old career and the dawn of my new one. She was a single mom, tough, hardworking—all the things you needed to be to raise a rebellious teenager who knew it all and didn't know anything at all. That's how she described her daughter the first time we met. The circumstances of our meet were anything but cute. It was horrific. Amber's daughter Pearl had been kidnapped walking home from school; her body dumped a day later in a culvert across town, strangled and mutilated beyond recognition. We never recovered the thin, gold necklace with a small piece of amber enclosed, the companion to her mother's necklace, a symbol of their bond. So, Amber held out hope it wasn't her. But there was a positive DNA match, and DNA never lies.

This case broke me.

Not long after, I moved to death investigation. As the city grew, so did my caseload. But I never forgot Pearl or Amber. After running into her at the police station a few times, I finally worked up the nerve to ask her out. It started with coffee, then dinner, then too many glasses of tannin-loaded wine and soft sobs of regret. Soon there was a place for my toothbrush and a drawer for my clothes. It might have been wrong, but the case was cold, and you couldn't deny a weather-worn investigator a few comforts in life. Amber and I got along fine, unless it was about her daughter. Every so often, in a fit of drunken stupor, she would blame me for not solving the case. And all I wanted to do was fix it. Because in truth, this case haunted my every waking moment; the way her body was twisted, the purplish tint of her skin, the smell.

Over the years, there were more missing teenagers with similar causes of death. Strangled and mutilated. They were scattered across the city, investigated by different precincts, different jurisdictions. I kept this information from Amber because I couldn't find a connection between the cases. I didn't see a point in dredging up her pain when there was no proof. But I had a suspect. An out-of-work tutor, a lonely man, good-looking, but eccentric.

Jacob Brown.

I could never forget that name. He tutored some of the girls, but not all. The medical examiner described the sort of knife used, and this guy was a washed-out military man. It didn't all fit, but I knew with time, and enough clues, it would. He would make a mistake; they always do.

And he did.

It was February 29th, leap year, and a full moon. Superstition ran high and the frenzy higher as they discovered the latest body. She had been dumped in a culvert, *the* culvert, where we found Pearl. Six years after Pearl's death, we had finally come full circle. Was it circumstance or merely coincidence?

This time around, I could only access the crime scene photos, yet every purple-tinted bruise, every laceration brought back memories of the smells and sounds of that day. The muted gags from seasoned veterans, the subtle gasps of horror from onlookers, the quiet clicks from my own camera. I could still feel the sun beating down my back, the heat penetrating my black windbreaker, streams of bright light against the vinyl *CSI* on my cap.

The medical examiner was thorough. His summary reported what I already knew. *Death by strangulation*, the mutilation occurred antemortem. Then, something caught my eye. Three lines down on the list of evidence collected from the decedent, below the usual fingernail scrapings and head hair combings, a bright blue check mark indicated apparent hairs and fibers were collected. Underneath that line in scrawling doctor's handwriting were the words *dark brown fibers*. I ran through my mental Rolodex, fingers already dialing the forensics laboratory.

"Mackenzie, please."

A short whir and a small click later, a gruff voice answered, "What?"

Professional as always.

"It's me, Nolan."

"Thought I was rid of you. What do you want?" Patrick Mackenzie, the smartest trace analyst I knew and the only trace analyst for our county. He was overworked, underpaid, and he liked it that way. The man never left the basement lab if he could help it, and no one wanted him to. He was an encyclopedia of fibers, probably wrote that encyclopedia himself.

"The fibers from the girl. Identify it yet?"

"What fibers from what girl?"

Playing coy, yet again.

"A bottle of Stoli jog your memory?"

"Throw in a large cheese pizza and maybe I'll remember."

What kind of psycho has pizza with vodka?

"Done."

"I want it still piping hot when it gets here."

"That's up to the pizza delivery guy."

"No, it's not. Personal delivery or you get zilch." This was serious. A personal delivery meant there were things he couldn't mention over the phone before he released the official report. "And extra cheese for being an asshole."

"I wasn't an a—" The line went dead. No use getting indignant with a guy like that; he simply didn't care.

The next phone call wasn't as pleasant. Word had gotten to Amber that we found another girl, teenaged and blonde, barely on the outskirts of sixteen. She had been trying to reach me and the unanswered calls only exacerbated her anxiety. She screamed, then sobbed, then whimpered. I consoled, cajoled, and finally promised I'd come home with some answers that night. Stupid, I know, but I felt Mackenzie was onto something big. Twenty-six years in the death business told me so.

Mackenzie's lab was exactly what you would expect from a basement-dwelling genius. Cold, sterile, with a mess of paperwork strategically strewn in all the right places. A string of microscopes lined the walls opposite a sagging bookshelf.

"Hey," I shouted, a bottle in one hand, an insulated bag in the other. A pair of magnified eyes popped out from under the desk.

"You got here quick." The scientist stood up, brushing dust off his red coveralls and removing the loupes from his head, indentations creasing his forehead and cheeks.

"Didn't want you to miss dinner."

"You look like shit." His eyes narrowed at my oversized shirt and rumpled khakis hanging off my wiry frame. I was never one for fashion, and I thought Mackenzie would be the last to judge.

"And you look like one of the mole people had a baby with Roger Rabbit," I shot back, running a hand through my graying hair; force of habit when I'm feeling self-conscious.

"I miss you too, Sunshine." He clamored for the bag, pulled the pizza box out and inhaled deeply. "You sure know the way to a man's heart."

"Not that I don't miss all the witty repartee, but can we get on with it? I don't want to miss my own dinner."

Mackenzie lifted a finger in between chews and motioned for me to follow. "The dark brown fiber our medical examiner pulled from the vic's body is none other than carpet fibers from a car, most likely the trunk."

My heart skipped a beat.

"We've never had fibers before?" It was more a statement than a question.

"Well..." the scientist gulped, "yes and no."

My ears perked.

Then began the longest two hours of my life. The plastic stool creaked under my behind, and I felt every bit my age as the scientist droned on. The main gist of it was, Mackenzie could now prove what I had suspected all along. Six years of murders, multiple girls, the same fibers collected in fifteen cases, filed away under different cause numbers, different labs in different counties. How did Mackenzie make the connection? One drunken poker night with four other fiber experts around the state. Months of examinations, tests, poking and prodding for confirmation.

"A Ford Mustang convertible, either a '67 or '68." Then he prattled on about the science behind matching carpet fibers, but I had heard enough. I knew one person in the vicinity who drove a car like that.

Amber was inebriated by the time I got home, blond hair bedraggled, shirt damp from crying, stained with half the bottle of wine she was sloshing around.

"Did you solve it yet?" She slurred, a glint of hope in her hazy eyes. I tried to steady her as she fell into my arms.

"How much have you had to drink?"

"Not nearly enough." The words rolled out heavy on her tongue. "You didn't answer my question."

"I have a lead," I mustered, "a strong one."

"Lead. To hell with the leads!" She screamed, chucking the wine bottle, nearly missing my head, wine and glass grazing my shirt as the bottle met the door. "I want answers. I want the bastard who did this to Pearl!" I tried to find sympathy tonight, but all I found was exasperation. My body tensed as I steeled myself against the barrage of insults sure to come next. Was I really an investigator, she asked, or just a useless vagrant using her home as a way station until my next stop? Was I here to alleviate her pain, or merely savoring it? I stood motionless at the front door as she hurled ridicule at me, wondering if it was time to walk out and leave her to her misery.

Then, as quickly as it came, the vitriol died down as she slumped against the wall in the foyer, her robe parting just enough for me to see the necklace. There would be no explanations tonight. I carried her to the bathroom, cleaned her, brushed her hair, and put her to bed. I placed two aspirin and a glass of water on the nightstand and retreated to the study.

I fished a file out from under the false bottom of the desk drawer and turned the pages, past the unsettling photos of Pearl's crime scene and straight to the medical report.

No fibers.

Then I pulled another file out.

Fibers.

On and on it went. Some had fibers, others didn't.

As a death investigator, we floated from one ADA to another. Any attorney that needed help could put in a request for one of us. However, in our down time, we could request assignments too, and that's exactly what I did. I made copies of everything I had access to, and for the ones I didn't, I called in favors, bargained and bribed until I had a complete set of every teenage murder around the state. It helped there were narrow parameters to work with; the only time I was thankful a serial killer had a modus operandi, a type, a perverse obsession. *But how did I miss the fibers?*

I stifled a yawn as the clock blared a blue five am. Twilight, a soft calm before the oncoming storm. When the human world was still mostly asleep, a quiet stirring alerted us to a shift change amongst nature's creatures. Nocturnal avians and mammals alike burrowed to rest while larks filled the morning air with a chorus of optimism.

There I sat with my puzzle. Some pieces fit; others didn't. It was enough, but not enough. Enough circumstantial evidence for a search warrant. Not enough for an indictment. And yet, smack dab in the middle of this web of conspiracy was one name.

Jacob Turling Brown.

"Hi." Her voice jolted me from my thoughts. It was quiet, yet tinged with guilt and a sharp sadness.

"Hi, coffee?" I asked, out of habit.

"Maybe later. What are you doing?" Her eyes rounded on the mass of papers surrounding my desk. At some point, I had given up on neatness; stacks of files and medical reports covered every surface of the room.

"Finding you answers."

She nodded slowly as I shoved some photos back in the blue folder, shielding her from their gruesome nature. She sat down in the small void I created with my hasty cleanup.

"I'm sorry."

"Don't be." I replied, mechanically. This was a dance we've done before. "I suppose you don't want breakfast either?".

"Later." She bit her lip. "Tell me."

I explained our findings, trying to keep it impersonal, professional, as if I were testifying in court. I couldn't afford to get emotional right now. We didn't have time to sit on the floor, to hold each other, to sob tears of grief and maybe relief. There was still work to be done. She interrupted me with questions, trying her best to be brave and to understand.

"What would the warrant do?"

"For starters, allow us to collect samples of the fibers from his car."

"And then, we've got him?" She was like a doe-eyed child, trying to skip to the end of the story.

"No," I shook my head and then quickly inserted, "but if it's a match, it'll get us another search warrant for his house."

"And what are you hoping to find?"

A pregnant pause. I didn't know if I should tell her this next part. "He keeps trophies, Amber." *Well, here goes nothing.* "Next of kin for a lot of these girls reported they were missing... *things*."

"What things?"

"Mostly jewelry or clothing." By clothing, I meant underwear, but I damn sure left that part out.

"And..." I hesitated, "a weapon."

"I thought they were strangled?" She asked, voice catching in her throat.

"Yes, but they were also," another pause, "hurt in other ways."

Her shoulders shook as the dam broke. "Who is he? Who did this to my baby?"

I fought the urge to reply. I wanted so badly to tell her, to end this nightmare for her, but I knew better. Some victims stayed still, meek, scared. But not Amber. Women like Amber would confront the problem head-on, lash out, *retaliate*.

"How did you do it?" I asked, hoping to distract her from the name.

"Do what?" She looked up, her irises almost periwinkle in the scattered light.

"Survive. All these years. Even before I met you, you were still working, doing things, searching for answers. Never letting anyone forget about Pearl or about the investigation."

She wiped her nose with the back of her hand. "Because I had hope."

"Hope for what?" I asked, confused.

She sighed, as if tired of explaining, though I've never asked before. "Hope that we would find the person responsible. Hope that we could bring them to justice."

The *we* hit hard. Did she mean me and her? Her and the detectives, the district attorney, the justice system?

"More than that, every day, I prayed she would walk through the door. That it was all a mistake. Maybe she was just tired of this life, of this town, maybe she ran away with a boyfriend or maybe she just got lost somewhere."

Hope is a silly thing. It's an illusion created by fragile, unrealistic people. From the beginning, we had established Pearl was not the type to 'run away' or 'get lost'. She was popular, well-liked by her peers and teachers. She wasn't into hard drugs or drinking. She led a low-risk life. Like normal teenagers, she fought with her mom and snuck out to parties. There were no dark secrets, no skeletons in her closet.

"What makes you think that?"

"I don't know. Maybe because I thought that as a teenager?" Amber was raised by a single mom in an abusive household. Her mother was always too doped up to know what her most recent boyfriend was doing to her daughter. There were no parallels to draw between their lives.

"C'mon. Let's get some coffee." I felt my knees creak as I got off the floor, holding an outstretched hand towards the crumpled figure next to me.

"What are you going to do next?" A chilling determination glazed her voice as she craned her neck to meet my eyes.

"A lot of things. I have prosecutors to rouse, warrants to file, answers to find." I lifted her from the floor. "But first, I want to have a cup of coffee with you." I needed the caffeine for all the work I was about to do, but I also needed her to see the mess she made, the mess she was inside. I needed her to get herself together because the next part was going to be rough.

The next few days were a whirlwind of actions and emotions. With Mackenzie's report concluding a case-to-case match of the fibers, I was able to nab a narrow search warrant from a lenient judge.

As I predicted, once Mackenzie declared the trunk fibers a match to at least three other cases, it gave us cause to cast a wider net. Jacob Brown's home, shed, and hunting cabin were searched. Not only did we find an old, World War 2 military blade that matched the wounds on some of the victims, but we also found a treasure trove of keepsakes.

I watched as the DA's Office of Special Investigations, along with agents from the state's bureau of investigation, walk the sick bastard across the courthouse steps through a myriad of flashing lights and noisy reporters. The case had gained so much media attention his trial had to be held in a county almost five hundred miles away to avoid jury bias. Amber was there every day during the trial, staring directly into his cold, steely eyes. He never broke a sweat, not even when they paraded his trophies out to the jury.

Stephanie O'Connell's Claddagh ring, an heirloom gift from her dying mother. Jessica Perry's birthstone necklace, a bright ruby encased in gold. A patch from Olivia Cornwall's letterman jacket, carefully sewn by her mother after she made it on the varsity swim team. Every piece of evidence was listed, displayed, personalized, endearing the victims to the jury, damning the monster sitting, recalcitrant, at the polished wooden table.

Amber stiffened as the prosecutors neared the end of the list.

Where was Pearl's necklace?

You see, as thorough as we were, we could only retrieve seven 'trophies', securing convictions for seven of the girls. To the DA, this was enough. He was gunning for the death penalty, and this was a sure thing. But the rest of the families could only drown in speculation of what happened to their daughters.

The investigation closed the day Jacob Turling Brown was convicted. The ordeal was over, done. Now was the time for grieving, burials, closure. No one was looking for the remaining items. I could see Amber shudder when the foreman read the guilty verdict out loud. As the courtroom broke into applause and emotional tirades, I saw her golden hair droop, shoulders go slack as her knees hit the floor. Pearl's murder had not been rectified. It wasn't over for her; it would never be.

I packed up the van the very next day; posted a for-sale sign on her yard, and we drove off, not knowing exactly where we were going or where we would end up. I just knew that we had talked about this plan for a long time, and by God, I was going to help her follow through.

As we finished lunch by the lake, I told her to go ahead to the car while I cleaned up. There was a cool breeze that day, and I had packed a picnic, figuring the calming waters would help her relax. I could see acceptance in her eyes as we talked it through. It's possible there was more than one hiding place for his trophies, we posited. It's possible he might have thrown some stuff away when we searched his car and he could see the writing on the wall, she reasoned. *Possible, possible, possible,* she murmured.

Acceptance.

"I hope our new place will have a lake this beautiful," she said, as she brushed dirt off her skirt.

"If that's what you want, I'll find a lake."

She smiled, a beautiful, daunting smile that slowly reached her eyes. Then she turned and walked towards the small parking lot, crossing the brush out of sight. I pulled a plastic bag from my windbreaker and toyed with the items inside one last time.

Claudia Gordon's sapphire earring, a graduation gift from her grandmother. A pair of pink underwear from Lisa Simmons. She didn't wear any jewelry, so there was nothing else to take. It was either this or a tooth, and collecting body parts was so crass. A lock of golden hair from Teri Lynn Swanson, curly and soft like Amber's. And finally, a small gold necklace with an enclosed chunk of amber that had caught my eye when it landed daintily at the crook of Pearl Banning's clavicle eight years ago. I rolled the gem between my fingers one last time before I let it all sink to the depths of the water.

Maybe hope wasn't an illusion after all. Because everything worked out just as I had hoped it would.

Survival of the Heart
by A. Hardy Roper (1st Place)

This story references child abuse and domestic violence that may be distressing or triggering for some readers. Reader discretion is advised.

C lara Gray stared at her buzzing cell phone, debating whether to answer. It was three o'clock on Friday afternoon, and she had just gotten her husband Jim and son Mark on the road for a Boy Scout camping trip. This was her weekend to relax—a Saturday morning latte at the coffee shop, a trip to the nail salon, and lunch with a friend. But her phone read CASA, and Clara knew something important was brewing because she'd never gotten a CASA call on a weekend.

As a volunteer for Court Appointed Special Advocates, Clara had just wrapped a year-long investigation involving a 13-year-old girl who had been sexually abused by her mother's live-in boyfriend. The girl had gone to her mother several times crying and begging for help. But the boyfriend was her mother's methamphetamine lifeline, and desperation trumped even her daughter's welfare. Due to Clara's dogged investigation, the court had terminated the mother's parental rights, and the girl was now living with an aunt in another county.

The case had been emotionally and physically exhausting, and she had told her supervisor she needed a break. She closed her eyes and tried to push away her growing frustration over receiving the call after she'd specifically said she needed time off. She decided to let the call go to voicemail. But her resolve melted when she listened to the message.

"Clara, this is Andrea at CASA. Sylvia Garcia with Child Protective Services called with a special case. Their caseworker, Gladys Hayes, had to take emergency leave due to pregnancy complications and the other caseworkers are swamped. She asked if CASA could assign a seasoned volunteer to a new case until a CPS agent could be freed up. I know you wanted a break, but the case involves a 14-year-old boy named Jesse Rucker and his mom, Annie. The boy is possibly being abused. Please call me."

When Clara heard "14-year-old boy," her heart melted. Her son Mark had just turned 14. She could only imagine....

Her mind flashed back to the tragedy of the 13-year-old girl in the case she'd just finished. If only someone had heard the girl's cries in time. But no one had, until the girl ran away and was picked up on the street by a police officer.

Clara listened to the message again, inhaled a deep breath and let it out slowly. She couldn't look away. She only hoped it wasn't too late for this boy.

She called Andrea, told her she would take the case and then buzzed Gladys Hayes, the caseworker now on maternity leave. Gladys answered on the first ring.

"Hi Gladys, this is Clara Gray. I am the CASA worker assigned to the Annie and Jesse Rucker case. I'm on the way for my first visit. Annie doesn't have a phone, so how do I let her know I'm coming?"

"You don't. Just show up and hope she's there," Gladys answered. "She's got a mobile home close to the national forest and works part-time at the Paper Moon, a beer joint down the road. She gets off at five and walks back to her digs in the woods. I only visited with Annie and Jesse one time before my doctor sent me home. Haven't been able to follow up on the investigation. Just hope the boyfriend, Skeeter Smith, isn't there. He looks like a real piece of work."

"Okay, thanks, Gladys. I got your report on the visit. Take care." Clara checked the time. If she hurried, she could still make her first visit today before dark.

Clara was the third generation of her family to call the small town of Loomis home. An old sawmill town, Loomis sat on the edge of the national forest. Clara loved the deep woods of the forest. She remembered the stories her grandfather had told her about the sawmills that dotted the area. Once as common as horseflies, he'd said. But that was before the national forest was created. Her grandfather had worked as the night cutter at a mill over at Minks Prairie, a company camp a few miles east of Loomis. Sadly, he'd lost his job when the mill closed, and he took to the bottle.

Sometimes, Clara thought drinking must be a kind of plague, as it seemed everyone in these woods had caught the disease. Bars and taverns were tucked away on every blacktop in the county.

On her way to Annie Rucker's mobile home, Clara thought about the eight-lane freeway that paralleled just east of the forest. People rushing by like shooting stars as though this was their last day on earth. They would never notice the early morning dew evaporating from the delicate redbud trees. They never saw armadillos rooting for their breakfast or a fawn suckling its mother. They could not know the sound of crows gathering by a small field, noising their way to dominance, or the pecking sound of the rare red-cockaded woodpecker echoing through the tall pines and breaking the morning silence. But more than any of this, if there was a small, lonely, human voice in the forest calling desperately for help, they would not hear it.

The sun was low in the sky when Clara reached the farm-to-market road leading to the mobile home. She knew the sun came late and left early in the deep woods. Along the road, broken rays of light struggled to reach the ground through the thick canopy of loblolly pines, hickory, and blackjack oak. In her youth, she had spent many pleasant hours hiking the forest trails. But she had never been comfortable in the woods after dark. A chill hit her bones as twilight closed in, causing eerie evening shadows to cover the entire two-lane.

She passed the Paper Moon, where Annie Rucker worked, the tavern's parking lot packed with old pickup trucks. A mile later she slowed as she approached the curve before the turnoff.

She glanced to her right, past the edge of the road. The heavy undergrowth hampered her view, but she knew the terrain sloped gently down to the creek-bed, the low area where primeval palmetto bushes provided an eerie prehistoric feel. It was as though the world had not changed for a hundred millennia. She shook off a chill, wondering if, at any moment, a great ancient beast might arise from the swamp, the master of its domain.

Clara turned onto the dirt road and stopped just short of Annie's mobile home. She bit down, trying to quiet her quivering lip. She blotted her forehead with a tissue and then leaned back against the seat, waiting for her heart to slow.

Why was she so damned nervous? During her five years as a volunteer for CASA, she had worked on many such cases. Most boiled down to physical or sexual child abuse due to druggie parents or live-in boyfriends. But no matter how many times she'd done this, the tension of the first call always sent her stomach fluttering.

Before she left home, Clara had reviewed the case file prepared by the caseworker, Gladys Hayes. While waiting to calm down, she removed the file from her briefcase and skimmed the relevant parts.

Jesse Rucker age 14. His teacher at Loomis Middle School called CPS with concern for Jesse's welfare...missing school and has lost weight. Before an above-average student, but recent grades had dropped precipitously...averts his eyes when spoken to (which is new)...has stopped associating with his classmates...seems nervous and distracted. He has also begun wearing long-sleeved shirts (even in warm weather) as if covering up some issue with his arms. The teacher thought it important to call CPS before school let out for the summer.

Mother: Annie Rucker, age31. Abused by a family member...ran away from home at age 16 pregnant with Jessee...moved in with her aunt who owned the mobile home where she and Jesse now live...aunt died when she passed out from drinking homemade dewberry wine, fell in her tomato patch and was bitten by a coral snake. A credit life policy on the mobile home paid off the trailer. Annie is currently involved in an on-and off-again relationship with Lloyd (Skeeter) Smith, age 42. Smith's sheet includes as-

sault on a police officer (one year in county jail) two DUI's, and six months in County for drug possession.

Clara worried about what she'd gotten herself into. Lloyd (Skeeter) Smith wasn't a man she wanted to meet by herself. But she couldn't stop thinking about Jesse and her own son, Mark, both 14. She knew she had to do what she could.

Clara moved her Jeep Cherokee slowly down the dirt road, barely able to see the mobile home through the thick yaupon undergrowth. She offered a silent prayer, thankful there was no vehicle in front. She knew Annie didn't have a car and Skeeter Smith drove a motorcycle.

A mud track bordered by uncut brush squeaked its way from the road to the house. She winced, visualizing each scratch in her side panels as she slugged past the brush, hoping a good wax job would remove the marks. Suddenly, the left front tire fell into a hole and her head flew forward. She held on tightly, narrowly avoiding crashing into the steering wheel. She straightened in the seat, revved the engine, and the rear tires pushed her forward.

Clara stopped at the end of the ruts, close to the rickety steps at the front of the mobile home. The trailer sat in a small clearing challenged by weeds and small trees. It was as though the forest was reclaiming the space, and there wasn't much time left before the takeover.

The mobile home sat on concrete blocks that had sunk unevenly into the mud, giving the home a sagging appearance. A rotting wooden porch provided just enough room for a dilapidated wooden table and two chairs. The aluminum door of the house stood partly ajar and bent in at the bottom, as though someone had kicked it open. Clara wondered if it would close and lock. The door's missing window had been replaced with taped cardboard. The window to the right of the door was also broken and patched. Streaks of dirt ran down the home's side.

Clara released her seat belt and looked up, murmuring softly, "Good God, my God. People live here?"

She cracked open the car door and closed it again quickly, sucking in a fast breath to the sound of a ferocious growl. At the corner of the house, a full-sized pit bull strained at its chain, vicious teeth pushing through its frothing mouth.

Not about to get out, Clara pressed hard on the horn. A slight, bare-footed woman, thin as a marsh reed and not five feet tall, appeared at the door wearing a wrinkled tank top and worn jeans. Long, stringy, unwashed blond hair, parted in the middle, hung past her shoulders. Clara noticed splotches marking her face and a dark bruise under her left eye.

The woman yelled down, "What you want?"

"I'm Clara Gray, the new caseworker taking Mrs. Hayes' place. Are you Annie?"

"Yeah, well shit. Don't worry, Buster's chained good. Come up to the porch and sit. I ain't got no air inside, too danged stuffy in there. Some-times we get a breeze out here."

Clara checked the dog again and eased up the stairs. Annie motioned to a seat at the table. She went inside and returned with two old jelly jars full of tepid water.

"Sorry it ain't cold, damned fridge shut down again."

Clara pretended to take a sip of water to be hospitable. "Is Jesse home from school?" she asked.

"This is the last bus stop. Be here soon."

"So, I am with CASA, Annie. Do you know about us?"

Annie frowned. "Well, some. CASA took a friend of mine's kids away. Her old man was a dealer. Got her hooked on coke, the sum bitch."

Clara waited to catch Annie's eye, which wasn't easy. "So, my job is to make sure Jesse is okay. To do that, I have to look into Jesse's life, and you and Skeeter are a part of that."

"Are ... are you going to take Jesse away?" Annie asked.

Clara caught the fear in Annie's eyes and the hesitation in her voice as she spoke. She waited a beat allowing Annie to get control. "I don't make that decision, Annie. The judge does. I file a report, including the facts I've found and my opinion. Part of that is seeing the way Jesse lives. Can we go inside so I can see his room?"

Clara noted the sink piled with dirty dishes and the crusted food parts lying splattered on the stovetop. An insect of some kind scurried past her on the floor.

Clara looked at Annie. "How do you keep food with the refrigerator out?"

"I got a cooler with ice on the back porch for Jesse's milk and such."

Clara stepped out onto the back porch and opened the cooler. An inch of water lay on the bottom, the residue of melted ice. She smelled the milk. "Best not to let Jesse drink this. Might make him sick."

Annie scrunched her face.

Clara knew the school provided breakfast and lunch for the students, but what about dinner? "What are you cooking tonight?" She fixed her eyes on Annie.

She answered softly, looking at the floor. "Beans and cornbread. Jesse likes his cornbread."

Clara moved to what passed as a cupboard. Inside was a half-full bag of pinto beans, an almost empty bag of rice, a box of saltine crackers and a jar of peanut butter. "How do you get groceries?"

"Friend of mine at the Paper Moon takes me when she's off."

"How long have you worked at the Paper Moon?"

"Couple of months, part-time. Easy walk, maybe a mile."

A musty odor reminiscent of smelly shoes hit Clara's nostrils as she entered Jesse's bedroom. The smell came from a sleeping bag piled on top of an old army cot and pushed against the wall. The only light came through a window with no covering. Clara saw no other furniture in the room and nothing mounted on the walls. She flipped the switch for the overhead light, and nothing happened.

"That dang bulb must be burnt out," Annie said. "I'll get a new one at the grocery store."

The small closet held the sum of Jesse's clothes: one pair of old jeans, two faded T-shirts and two long-sleeved shirts. No shoes. Clara turned to the sound of a boy's voice in the living room.

"Mama, you here? Whose car's outside?"

Clara followed Annie to the living room. Jesse's arms remained lifeless at his sides as Annie hugged him. Clara noticed the gesture of protection as Annie kept her arm around Jesse when she moved him toward her.

"Jesse, this is Miss Clara. She wants to meet you."

Jesse seemed to shrink against his mother's side.

Clara stepped forward, smiling. "Hi Jesse. I am with CASA. Do you know about us?"

Jesse's eyes bounced around the room. "Yeah, I know some. You took a kid at school away from his mama. You ain't gonna take me. I won't go." He turned and started for the door.

"I'm just here to talk," Clara said to Jesse's back. "Let's go outside." Clara motioned for Annie to stay back.

Clara followed Jesse out to the porch, where he sat on the steps facing the road.

"I'm here to be your friend. One of your teachers at school was worried about you and called us. My job is to check on you, see how things are going."

Jesse didn't respond. He lay back on the steps, resting on his elbows and looking out at the forest away from Clara.

She waited a beat. "Jesse, it would help if you would talk to me."

"I ain't gonna leave my mama," he said, still looking away. "She needs me."

"Tell me about that."

Jesse didn't answer for what seemed like a couple of minutes. Finally, he turned to her. "That bastard, Skeeter. He comes 'round and...."

"And...?"

"Mean, hits her. Hits her a lot. She's scared of him. I keep telling her let's leave, get away, go someplace. She won't do it." Jesse turned back, eyes downcast.

Typical battered woman syndrome, Clara thought. Skeeter had probably pounded Annie's already low self-esteem, telling her how worthless she was. And she had bought into it.

Clara's stomach roiled in protest, but she needed to keep her cool. Keep Jesse involved.

"Is he mean to you, too, Jesse?"

No response.

Clara laid her arm softly on Jesse's shoulder. "You can tell me, Jesse."

Jesse whimpered softly. He scooted down a step away from her arm. He wiped his eyes with his hand and turned.

Clara met his eyes. She waited, holding her breath, hoping she'd reached him.

Jesse slowly rolled one sleeve up and then the other. Purple bruises covered both arms. "Belt."

Clara frowned and looked closer. She scrunched her eyes in disbelief at what appeared to be burn marks. 'Is that...? Is that a...?"

Jesse nodded. "Cigarette when he was drunk." His face turned red; anger flared in his voice. He balled his hands into fists and shook them, fire in his eyes. "I wanted to kill the bastard."

Clara wanted to hug Jesse and not let go, but she knew she hadn't reached that point of intimacy. She felt helpless, couldn't think of anything to say. She sat with Jesse for a few more moments, both silent, staring out into the woods.

Finally, she rose and gave Annie and Jesse her business card and told them she would be back tomorrow. On her way home, she called Sylvia Garcia, the CPS supervisor, on the case. She relayed everything that had happened at Jesse's mobile home.

"Good God, this is a bad one," Sylvia offered. "We need to act."

"I told them I'd be back tomorrow."

"I'll go with you."

Clara thought this may be her worst case yet. What kind of animal would burn a child with a cigarette? She nervously tapped the steering wheel, worried about waiting until tomorrow morning. What if Skeeter came back tonight?

She stopped at a small Italian kitchen close to her house for a salad and glass of wine. Clara couldn't let go of what she'd seen and heard at the trailer. She didn't have the authority to remove Jesse from his home. That was up to CPS. But she would do everything she could to get Jesse out of there.

She decided she would call Sylvia back after dinner and see how early they could go tomorrow. She sipped her wine, closed her eyes and tried to relax, pushing away her worried feelings.

Halfway through the meal, her phone buzzed. She recognized the area code but not the number. Another spam call? She usually didn't answer if the caller wasn't in her contact list, but she had just given Annie and Jesse her number.

"Hello?"

Sobbing.... Heavy breathing.... "It's Jesse." More panting like he was out of breath. "He...he came back...hurt Mama bad."

Clara rose quickly, threw money on the table and hurried outside. "Are you hurt?"

Jesse stammered, "He...he slapped me, but I'm okay."

"Was Skeeter still there when you left?"

"No, he's gone, took his dog. But Mama's hurt bad. I ran all the way to the Paper Moon. Mama's friend Tye let me use his phone."

Clara took a deep breath, heart pounding. She needed to stay focused, to keep her composure.

"Okay. Listen, Jesse. I am calling an ambulance and the police now. You stay at the Paper Moon. I'm on my way to get you. Don't worry, your mama will be fine. Just stay there, okay?"

Clara disconnected, called 911and gave Annie's address and the need for EMS and the police. She hung up and called Sylvia Garcia.

After a hurried explanation, Sylvia's words exploded out of the phone, "Don't go back there alone. Come to my house. We'll take my car."

Ten minutes later, Clara met Sylvia outside her house. Sylvia looked early 40s, maybe five or so years older than herself, with long dark hair that fell below her shoulders. They jumped into Sylvia's Mustang and, minutes later, raced down the farm road toward Annie's mobile home. Through the night haze, Clara caught the glare of the lights from the Paper Moon. Sylvia squealed into the lot and slammed on the brakes. The front door of the bar opened, and a man stepped out with his hand on Jesse's shoulder.

"I'm Tye, the owner here."

In a sudden burst, Jesse ran to Clara, tears streaming down his tortured face. He threw his arms around her waist. Clara held him tight.

Sylvia nodded to Clara. "You stay with Jesse. I'm going to Annie's, be back as soon as I can."

Clara sat beside Jesse on a bench at an outdoor table. She put her arm around him. He laid his head on her shoulder, crying. After a minute, he stopped and straightened on the bench. She gave him a tissue to wipe his eyes and cheeks.

"I shoulda killed that bastard like I said."

Clara turned sideways to face Jesse. She waited until he raised his eyes to hers and, with as much firmness as she could muster, she said, "You will never see Skeeter again."

A few minutes later, the EMS ambulance roared by the Paper Moon toward town, lights flashing and siren blasting. A sheriff's car followed. Then Sylvia's Mustang slid into the bar's parking lot. She got out and went to Clara and Jesse.

"Your mom is going to be okay, Jesse. EMS is taking her to the hospital. She'll be there a couple of days while they check her out. A lady from Adult Protective Services will meet us at the hospital. Her job is to make sure your mom is taken care of. She has a special place where your mom can live and feel safe. It's called a women's shelter, and there are other women there in the same situation."

"I will go with her?" Jesse asked, hope in his eyes.

"Not right away," Sylvia answered. "Our job is to make sure you are safe and taken care of. We will take you to the hospital so you can see your mom, and then Miss Clara and I will take you to a home where there are other boys your age. You will be safe there."

"But I want to be with Mama!"

"I know you do, Jesse. And we want that, too. Miss Clara will be checking on you regularly and giving you updates. She will be helping you in every way she can. You trust Miss Clara, don't you?"

Jesse nodded.

"Meanwhile, you'll stay at a new place. You'll go back to the same school. And you will have regular visits with your mom while she's working things out."

While Jesse visited his mom at the hospital, Clara and Sylvia took a moment to reflect on the situation.

"Not living with his mother will be hard on Jesse," Clara frowned. "Are you going to file against Annie?"

"I have to," Sylvia concluded. "Neglectful Supervision and Termination of Parental Rights. I can't allow Jesse to continue living with Annie. You saw the squalor they live in. No food, no refrigeration. Electricity will be cut off soon. Did you see his filthy sleeping bag? My God...."

Clara lowered her head and rubbed her eyes, as if hoping things would be different when she opened them. After a moment of silence, she spoke, a wistful look on her face. "Tell me about the Ellsworth Group Home."

"They're good folks, running the home for ten years. Currently have seven boys, aged 10 to 16, can handle eight. They agreed to take Jesse on an emergency basis."

When Jesse came out from visiting his mom, the three of them piled into Sylvia's Mustang. Twenty minutes later, they drove into the Ellsworth yard.

Clara smiled at Jesse. "Nice skate park and basketball court, huh?"

Jesse didn't answer.

The door to the house opened, and Dave and Sandy Ellsworth greeted Jesse with broad smiles. "Welcome to our home, Jesse," Dave said. "We are glad you will be staying with us."

Inside, the home was set up with an apartment-style living area at one end for the Ellsworths, then a great room with couches and small tables containing various games. A large TV hung on the far wall. Next to the living area was the kitchen with two tables and chairs, and then the bathroom and two bedrooms with bunk beds.

Dave Ellsworth motioned Jesse forward. "The boys are in their rooms getting ready for bed. Are you hungry, Jesse?"

Jesse's eyes drifted away as he answered, his hands by his side squeezing into fists and releasing again. "No, sir. We ate at the hospital."

Sylvia had quickly gathered a sack containing Jesse's clothes before leaving the mobile home. She handed it to Dave. "Not much in there."

"No worries," Dave noted. "We've got it covered."

"What about my...my mama?" Jesse stammered, a squeak in his voice. "When will I see her again?"

Clara sat on a couch and motioned for Jesse to sit next to her. "I'll pick you up tomorrow and take you to the hospital. When your mom's okay, she'll go to the women's shelter. This arrangement is up to Child Protective Services and the court, so I don't know how long it will go on. But you and your mom will be safe, and you will see your mom often. Meanwhile, you'll live here and go to school."

Jesse hung his head and cupped his face in his hands. He took a couple of deep breaths, then looked up at Clara.

"I guess I understand ... it's okay, Miss Clara. Thank you."

Later that night, Sylvia called Clara at home. "Sheriff's deputies picked up Skeeter Davis in a bar. Arraignment in the morning. I'm hoping the judge sets bail high enough to keep him in jail."

"That would be a blessing."

"I'll have a new caseworker assigned as soon as possible. CPS will get a court order for Temporary Managing Conservatorship. Meanwhile, Clara, you are Jesse's Guardian Ad Litem, the 'eyes and ears' of the judge, as the saying goes."

"So, the court will order the usual Family Plan of Services for Annie?"

"It's CPS's goal to reunite families when possible." Sylvia sighed. "She'll have to prove herself a capable parent. Steady housing and income, parenting classes, psych evaluation, and random UA tests for drugs. It will take a while."

"I think she'll do it. She loves that boy. Dave Ellsworth called me on my way home. He said Jesse's bunkmate is a boy Jesse knows from school.

He said the boy plays the saxophone in the school band and he's talking to Jesse about joining. Dave said when he was making the last bed check, he listened at the door and heard them giggling.

Sylvia laughed. "Well, it's a start. How are you feeling about this, Clara?"

"Sad, but also relieved. I think we rescued Jesse and Annie just in time."

"Sometimes we get lucky."

"What about therapy?" Clara asked.

"I'll recommend it for both. It will help, but they have a long way to go."

"I feel for Jesse. He's been through hell."

"Yes, but children are resilient. They adapt. They have to—for survival."

After the call, Clara poured a glass of her favorite red wine and retreated to the sofa in her living room. It had been a tough night, and she was ready for Jim and Mark to come home. She needed a hug and the simple reassurance that her family was intact. She set the glass on the coffee table, leaned back against the sofa and closed her eyes, her mind drifting to what special dish she would prepare for dinner Sunday evening.

If you enjoyed this book, please consider leaving a review at your favorite book site. Reviews help other readers find and enjoy new books!

About the Authors

Denise Bossarte ("The Robot and the Green Dragon")

Denise Bossarte is an award-winning author, poet, photographer, and artist whose passion is inspiring others. Her daytime job in IT helps to keep the household running. She enjoys writing, teaching contemplative photography workshops, and going on photo shoots to discover the extraordinary in the ordinary world. She teaches and photographs near her home in Texas. Denise is a member of the International Thriller Writers and an affiliate member of the Horror Writers Association for her works in the Grace Bishop Paranormal series.

Ian Ehrhart ("Odd Behaviors")

Ian is an elementary school paraprofessional in Houston, Texas, who loves reading fantasy and mystery novels. He has a degree in general arts from Lone Star Cy-Fair, and is going back to school to get his B.A. in creative writing at UHD, so he can become a teacher. He enjoys playing video games, trying out new restaurants, and traveling the world.

Tassie Kalas ("It Takes a Village")

Tassie writes short stories about marriage, motherhood, dog hair, and divorce. Her debut book, Yaya's Big Black Purse: Drama of a Greek Mama, was a finalist in the Story Circle Network Gilda Book Award competition for humor. Her stories have appeared in Chicken Soup for the Soul: Age is Just a Number, and Laugh Out Loud, 40 Women Humorists Celebrate the Then and Now...Before We Forget, an anthology which was named a finalist for one of the best humor books of 2019 by the Next Generation Indie Books Awards program. She loves outdoor patios, frozen margaritas, and making people laugh. Through the bittersweet journey of life, she still believes in happily ever laughter—and hopes you do, too.

Kyle McKee ("Arman and Armageddon")

Kyle is a novelist with a love for fantasy, comedy, and horror. Born and raised in Texas, he now spends his days with his wife and two daughters, lovingly nicknamed Shiv and Scar. When he's not daydreaming of swinging a sword at eldritch horrors, he enjoys playing tabletop games, practicing martial arts, and cooking.

Kristin Marie Mitchener ("Threads")

Kristin is a fifth-generation Texan and third-generation south-paw. A lover of writing and books from a young age, Kristin's earliest memories are of assembling scraps of newspapers and magazines to create masterpiece publications and of being curled up with a smelly library book, her favorite being Stuart Little by E.B. White. In her teen years, Kristin began writing more intentionally as a way of both escaping and making sense of her chaotic home life with her emotionally absent mother. Purposeful in her vulnerability, she details the lifelong effects of childhood trauma and how healing from this trauma is possible. She is a member of Writespace, a grassroots literary arts organization in Houston, Texas, where she resides with her husband, Preston, and their rescue chihuahua-terrier, Kingston.

A.V. Pham ("Keepsakes")

A.V. spends her days dissecting crimes in the lab—and her nights inventing savvier ways to commit said crimes. With her case files in tow, she sets out to spin twisty tales wrought with witty dialogue, dark humor, and just enough weird to keep it interesting. Fueled by caffeine and chocolate donuts, she's on a mission to prove that real life is indeed stranger than fiction ... but fiction is way more fun.

A. Hardy Roper ("Survival of the Heart")

Hardy is a fourth-generation Houstonian who writes from a wealth of knowledge about the area's storied past and vibrant present. Hardy has written and published five novels, all based on Galveston Island, where his intrepid protagonist, Parker McLeod, rescues friends and battles evil. The books in order of publication are: The Garhole Bar, Assassination in Galveston, Saving Jake, Bad Moon Rising, and his latest: Girls Lost, which tracks the kidnapping of two teenage girls by human traffickers. After retiring from the insurance business, Hardy—along with his lovely wife, Winkie—returned to his beloved Heights, where he grew up. Hardy continues to write and is currently working on his next novel.

K.M. Sokulski ("I Am the Monster in the Closet")

K.M., A.K.A. Karina Michele Sokulski, writes stories about bravery, humanity, and monstrosities. While Karina always had a love for the most complex, fantastical, horrifying, and tragic of stories, she didn't seriously consider publishing her work until she interned at her first publishing house. Karina published her first short story, "Shoes," in The Barker's Voice: A Journal of Arts & Letters. Karina published her second short story, "Jexa," in the Houston Writers Guild's Journey Into Time anthology. Thanks in no small part to her fabulous critique group, Karina is currently working on her first fantasy and horror novel series. Karina hails from Katy, Texas, where she lives happily married with the love of her life, a deeply fabulous cat, an exceptionally affectionate dog, and her startlingly photogenic first child.

Ricki Wegner ("The Gift of the Trees")

Rickie is a healthcare worker by day, and a writer by night. She uses her unique experience as a healthcare worker, humanitarian worker, and writer to explore the human experience through poetry, stories, fables, and fairy tales.

Cyndi Whatif ("Stupid Little Word")

Cyndi writes short stories, memoirs, and nonfiction. She is a relentless seeker of knowledge who has lived more than fourteen years past her "expiration date." She spent five years developing her hypothesis about a newly revealed body system, and another five years testing it. She now writes about her discovery under the pen name Cyndi Whatif, a name inspired by the many questions she still has and the countless possibilities this system could impact.

www.ingramcontent.com/pod-product-compliance
Lightning Source LLC
Chambersburg PA
CBHW071126250626
47159CB00006B/2151